# MOONSHINER IN TRAINING

## SAM PEMBERTON

Publishing Coordinator – Sharon Kizziah-Holmes

Paperback-Press
an imprint of A & S Publishing
Paperback Press, LLC
Springfield, Missouri

ISBN -13: 978-1-960499-95-0

# DEDICATION

To the characters in this series of books, family, friends and fictitious, thank you for allowing me to tell the stories.

# ACKNOWLEDGMENTS

Once again, I'd like to thank those who help me most when I'm putting these stories together.

Pat, you're the best proofreader I've ever had. Thank you for bearing with me through the process of all this. I couldn't do it without you or your eagle eye. Plus, I kinda like ya'.

L. Kennedy, you have done another bang up job on editing. You don't know how much I appreciate your hard work.

Thanks to you, Sharon Kizziah-Holmes, for always putting together a stellar book. You do a great cover, and the interior design is just what I want. You're the best.

# PREFACE

Carl Harris was a young man on his own after he decided not to go with his dad and sister to Oklahoma. At fourteen years old he was mature beyond his years. Suffering through the loss of his mother and a sister along with the hardships of being responsible for the farm forced him to become a man.

After a trip to Cozy looking for work, he returned to the house where he had lived since, he was four years old. He decided to leave after learning his father sold the homestead. Planning to retrieve a bow and arrow set from the attic of the house was his only reason for returning.

It was too late, because the house was on fire. Desperate, lonely, and confused he slept the night in the yard and then decided to go up Big Creek looking for work.

"Willie Sitton will hire you when you get to the bridge" a constant message from everyone he asked about work. The story really begins when he joins Willie Sitton, the moonshiner.

Carl Harris becomes a "moonshiner in training."

# CHAPTER 1

It was still dark when Carl Harris was awakened by the sound of the cedar trees. It wasn't wind. It was the dripping of water from the limbs. There was a heavy mist falling. Low clouds had moved in during the night while he slept in the yard. He had seen it happen several times during the years he had lived in the hollow. The afternoon before as he walked home, there was smoke in the distance. The smoke was coming from the direction of the house where his family had lived since moving to Arkansas from Mississippi. A spiral of black smoke replaced the white billows as he left the trail and began running through the woods toward his home. When he got to the fire, the only building burning was the house. He was confused and devastated as he watched the house continue to burn. A feeling of being helpless replaced fear as he wandered around the yard.

Even with the early morning rain, the smoldering embers were still burning and creating steam rising into the fog. The fire had burned all night. The place had been his home since he was seven years old. He wondered why anybody would burn the house.

Carl lay still while watching the smoke and steam rising from the embers. Looking around the yard, without the house, the barn and chicken coop looked out of place. He wasn't anxious to get out of his bed because the quilt was warm and comfortable. The bed was a camping quilt his mother made for him when he was nine years old. Raising up on his elbow, he looked around and tried to remember why he camped in the yard of his home. There wasn't an answer to the question. Well, now his home was gone. Carl was alone. He was fourteen years old. A grown man, maybe, He had stopped growing in height at just over 5'8" tall. He hadn't grown any since he turned twelve. Black hair with a dark complexion accented by the heavy muscles developed while doing farm work. After his mother became ill, he was responsible for taking care of the farm. His father spent his time caring for his mother. Carl tried to remember how many days had passed since she died.

During his mother's sickness, Carl had watched as his dad suffered through several losses. He went to Mississippi and got four young heifers. Which were prize breeding stock. When they went missing, the heifers showed up in Coy Bryant's corral at his barn on Big Creek. Coy claimed he bought the heifers in Missouri but didn't have a bill of sale. Carl's dad made several trips to the Sheriff in Searcy County, but no one would believe they were his livestock. He didn't have a bill of sale either because his family in Mississippi gave them to him as a gift. The sheriff refused to believe his story.

Carl would have gone with his dad and sister if they had returned to Mississippi, but they decided to go to Oklahoma instead. After they left, Carl went to see Paul Avey at Cozy. He had to have a job If he was going to stay in Arkansas. Paul recommended Carl go up Big Creek looking for work.

"You may have to go all the way to the farms up around Campbell, but someone will let you work for them," Paul said.

Carl stopped by the McClung's place in Turkey pen hollow as he was returning from Cozy. They told him his dad sold his place to Fred Hudson. He was not interested in working for Fred Hudson. Carl gave his dog to Mr. McClung. He wouldn't be needing a dog with him while he was looking for work. The decision was made. He would go up Big Creek to look for work. Before he left looking for work, he decided to get a bow and arrow set stored in the attic of the house. They were given to him by his grandfather when he was six years old. They were the only things he owned from his family in Mississippi. After getting them, he would be ready to leave. He would go anywhere away from Coy Bryant's farm and the place where his family was buried.

While watching the house burning, he thought" it's just as well, it will put an end to the memories". He would never know why he decided to unfold his backpack and camp in the yard. The backpack held all of his belongings and was a special quilt that his mother made him for camping. It was thick with three layers of canvas stitched together with heavy stitching. His mother called the stitching "tack stitching". The fringe around the camping quilt was laced with leather. There were loops ten inches apart and straps threaded through them which made a sleeping bag. It took some time for his mother to explain how to convert the backpack into a sleeping bag. While lying on the quilt, the sides could be pulled up and laced together., but he had to learn how to do it correctly. When he did it right, the sleeping bag was a comfortable bed. She also showed him how to put all his gear inside and turn it back into a backpack.

He left the farm with the quilt as a backpack secured with loops over each shoulder. He still didn't know why he unpacked and camped in the yard after he got back and discovered the fire. It was cold and miserable when he got up. He walked closer to the smoldering coals. He stood and was warmed by the fire. The logs were still burning. He walked around to where his mother's grave was marked by a crude stone with nothing carved on. He paused momentarily and went back to where he had slept. He packed his things and decided it was time to walk away and forget about where he lived for half of his life.

# CHAPTER 2

The last week of March was ushering in spring. Despite the cold, the buds on the trees were bursting with growth as they became leaves. Carl was following the path along the edge of the bluff. Walking along the path beside the corral reminded him of the morning his dad came running back to the house, yelling "the heifers are gone". The four heifers were given to his dad by their family in Mississippi. As he looked at the empty corral, he remembered that day as the day his dad's spirit was broken. Carl's spirits improved the farther he got from the cabin. The leaves were barely visible at the end of the limbs and did not cast a shadow over the path. The morning sun did not create a shade and felt good as the fog was lifting. The morning was becoming warmer.

The memory of the day the heifers went missing was the strongest memory Carl was carrying with him. He remembered how the search started immediately. They followed the tracks of the heifers along the path away from the corral. Carl walked below the trail and his dad walked above it. They began to see boot prints mixed in with the tracks of the cattle.

"Someone is driving the calves!!" He remembered his dad saying constantly as they followed the tracks.

"If they weren't being herded together, they would be forging on the grass and not staying in the path." His dad added.

The discussion continued as they followed the trail until the boot prints disappeared. They were replaced by two sets of horse tracks mixed in with the hoof prints of the cattle.

"Dad, there's no way of knowing where the horses came from or if they are following the cattle," Carl remembered saying as they followed the ledge around the west bluff above Big Creek. They came out of a glade where a cabin was being built. There were three sides to the cabin.

"This is where that railroad worker is building his cabin," Carl's dad commented.

There was no one around. They stepped up on a big rock and looked below the bluff where Coy Bryant's big barn with its corrals was located. The barn had four corrals, and another one was being built. There were livestock in the corrals. After pausing for a short time, they continued following the tracks of the four heifers; two more horses had joined the trail. The riders of the horses were alternating with one of them in the trail and the others leaving from time to time. They followed the horses tracks and the cattle tracks off the bluff and along the west side of Big Creek.

Carl remembered they lost the track at the mouth of Big Creek where it joined the Buffalo River. They searched both directions along the river several times but never picked up the trail. The river was too full for them to cross. He didn't remember what they did when they gave up the search.

Carl stopped thinking about that day. He didn't recall much about losing the cattle until his dad came home from visiting with the railroad worker who was building the cabin. He remembered his dad telling the story to his mother about seeing the heifers in Coy Bryant's corral. They had stood on the rock at the edge of the bluff where they could clearly see the cattle. The railroad worker joined him, and they went to the corral. Seth Tabor was new to the community and had never seen the cattle, but Carl's dad was sure it was the stock he brought from Mississippi. The memory faded as Carl descended from the bluff to the banks of Big Creek.

Carl walked on the west side of Big Creek. He wasn't sure where he was going. He was going to follow the creek and check with farmers until someone let him go to work for them. He had salt, a skillet, a .22 caliber rifle, fishhooks with fishing line, and matches for starting a fire in the backpack. At just fourteen years old, he had developed a lot of survival skills, and he could survive.

Crossing the creek was easy when he came to a place where rocks extended across the lower end of a hole. The creek had cleared up enough that he could see several smallmouth bass swimming in the deep water. The fish would be a nice start for his supper. He caught four fish just before dark. They were cooked by threading the fish on a stick and roasting them over his campfire to a golden brown. They were delicious, and he wouldn't starve.

The fish was a good start to surviving on his own, but it wasn't possible for him to live off the land. He was anxious to find a place where he could work and live permanently. Once again, he made camp by unfolding the backpack and creating a bed. The sticks from the campfire were used to support the tent portion of the sleeping bag which would cover his head. A slight mist had continued all day, and it was falling as he lay down. He wasn't lonesome or scared, he just knew he had to keep going to survive.

# CHAPTER 3

Placing the .22 caliber rifle alongside the bedroll and covered it with the flap and before laying down. The gravel bar was clean in the area he chose to make camp. The gravel was close to the same size and made a much better spot to sleep than areas with large rocks. When he first started camping, he discovered it was not a good idea to spread the bedroll over different sized rocks, as the larger ones became very uncomfortable during the night.

The usual noises began as soon as he laid down. There was an owl screeching, plus a whippoorwill starting his night call. The whippoorwill was being answered by another one high on the hill above the bluff. Listening to the sounds didn't bother Carl. A loud splashing sound came from the creek, —it was a mink catching its evening meal. All the sounds were things he recognized from camping before. He went to sleep.

Carl was awakened by the sound of someone walking in the creek gravel. When he opened his eyes and looked out from under his makeshift tent, he was staring up at a huge man he had never seen before. As he was rising out of the bed, the man came closer.

"You that Harris boy?" the man asked.

Carl was startled before he answered "Yeah," and then added, "How'd you know?"

"I watched you yesterday, while you were catching your fish for dinner," the man answered.

Carl got up. He folded the tent portion of the sleeping bag underneath and began placing the rest of his belongings inside to make the backpack. The large fellow stood with hands on his hips and did not comment while he watched Carl packing up his belongings.

After Carl had finished, he asked, "Where are you headed, son?"

Carl answered," I don't know."

He walked around his backpack and made sure he was not leaving anything, then laid his gun across the backpack.

"I'm headed up Big Creek until I find a place to work," Carl added while walking between the man and the creek.

The man stuck out his hand, "I own the Morrow place, here where you are camped." As they shook hands, he added, "My friends call me Cal."

Carl felt at ease. He knew Mr. Morrow didn't mean any harm.

They both stood on the creek bank. A stone-toter fish was carrying pebbles and placing them in a circle to make a bed for laying eggs. The fish always worked hard for several days to create a place to lay their eggs. The male fish carried the stones, and the female fish fanned them into place with her tail fin before laying her eggs. The male fish would fertilize them before he brought in the last layer of stones.

How long they stood watching, neither Carl nor Mr. Morrow knew. It was fascinating to observe.

Mr. Morrow finally commented, "I watch them do this every spring." He walked toward where the fish were building their bed. "I used to wonder how they figured out the right place to put the bed for their hatch. I have checked after a flood, and they stay intact and don't wash out."

Carl was following along behind Cal, listening to his description of the location the fish had chosen. He had noticed the same things before about fish in the spring in Big Creek. The smallmouth bass always fanned out the gravel to create a bed for their spring hatch, and they also chose places that would survive the spring floods.

"One year I decided to cut four trees above the next hole of water and make some post for fence, and the fish built their bed in the same spot as the year before." He pointed up the creek. "I can show you the spot where that happened, when the spring flood came the treetops changed the flow of the creek and wiped out the fish beds. They knew what to expect if I had left the flow of the creek alone." Mr. Morrow stopped the story and turned toward Carl to ask, "You want to go to my house for breakfast?"

He didn't wait for Carl's answer. He picked up the backpack and handed the gun to Carl. He walked away, with Carl following.

Carl wondered how he knew who he was and how he knew the circumstances of his leaving after the house burned. He assumed he knew his mother and little sister were buried in the yard. Carl didn't ask any questions, he just followed until they passed a big log barn on the right and were looking at the front of a huge log house with a porch all the way around and a hallway running two directions, separating the house into four separate rooms.

Carl had heard stories about the Morrow man who built four log cabins and covered them with one roof and a porch all the way around. Now he was seeing the house firsthand and remembered the day a neighbor came by their homestead and asked his dad if they had ever been to Cal Morrow's place.

"The best molasses I've ever eaten came from the

Morrow place," was the way his dad answered the question. Carl assumed he was following the same man to his house for breakfast.

# CHAPTER 4

They went into the barn before stopping. Cal Morrow turned and said to Carl, "I need to throw out some hay for the horses and a couple of steers.

Carl watched as Mr. Morrow climbed the ladder into the barn loft. The ladder entered the loft in the middle of a long hallway. While he was throwing out hay, Carl looked at the walls of the barn hallway. Six feet above the ground, there was a cedar log mixed in with the oak. The cedar tree must have been huge. The cedar log had been flattened on two sides to fit into the wall. The log extended out past the one above and below it, creating a shelf. There were limbs left on the log that were cut back to about six inches in length. The limbs created hangers for farm gear to be hung in the hallway. Carl was amazed. He had not seen a cedar log used to create hangers before.

Several of the homesteads in the area had cedar posts for their porches. Typically, limbs were left for hanging stuff on the porch. Carl remembered his dad remarking "It has to be something to do with these people from Wayne County, Tennessee." They visited a couple of neighbors and found everything imaginable hanging from the porch post.

Those porches look cluttered. The log in the hallway of Mr. Morrow's barn was neat. There were harnesses for horses hanging according to size. The collars were hanging over limbs which had been padded to protect their shapes. By the time Mr. Morrow climbed back down and returned, Carl had made a mental note of the hallway and if he ever built a barn of his own it would have a log with limbs for hanging harness and equipment.

"I am going to starve us to death and breakfast is going to be cold," Mr. Morrow said, and took off at a pace that required Carl to almost jog to keep up.

They went up the steps in the center of the porch. They were on the north side of the house and there were not any doors to enter the two rooms on each side of the hallway. They went to the center of the house. Where the two hallways intersected, there was a water well directly in the center, with a bucket and rope for drawing water.

"That's a spring." Mr. Morrow pointed to the bucket and the rock circling the well. Carl leaned over and peered into the well. He could hear the water running and could see the ripples of light on the water.

"Where does the water go?" he asked, peering into the well.

"I'll show you after breakfast. Let's go inside and see what is ready to eat," Mr. Morrow said.

Carl followed him into the southeast portion of the house. The entire opposite wall from the door was a rock structure. There was a cookstove sitting on the rocks with a pipe running into the rock above a large fireplace. The fireplace had four logs burning with a low flame coming out between the logs. The room was cozy. There was a loft along two walls with ladders at each end and a rail between the ladders. Carl could not see what was in the loft. Mr. Morrow touched

Carl's shoulder. He pointed to a table set up between the fireplace and another larger table.

"We will eat there," Mr. Morrow said as Carl followed him and sat in the chair that a younger boy pulled out for him.

Carl looked around the room. There were two women busy placing food on the tables. There were girls seated at a table across the room from where Carl was seated.

He had been too busy observing the surroundings to notice the food.

"Let us pray." Mr. Morrow bowed his head and prayed a rather loud and long prayer. When he finished the prayer everyone, but Carl said "Amen".

Carl was embarrassed and was sure that he had never been around a family comparable to the Morrows. The most interesting contact with a family had occurred since he was standing in the hallway of the barn and during the time he was coming to the big house and was seated at the table for breakfast, he was overwhelmed trying to observe all the things he'd never seen before.

After the prayer, breakfast began. There was a pile of biscuits on one tray, and sausage, bacon and ham on another.

"Do you want any eggs?" Mr. Morrow asked. "We cooked those as we eat them. I don't like cold eggs." Carl answered the question about eggs by eating three cooked well done.

Breakfast was over quickly. Carl followed Mr. Morrow as he led him out the west side of the house. When they arrived at the hollow that ran behind the big barn there was a stream coming from the direction of the house.

"That's the spring we draw the water from on the porch." Mr. Morrow pointed back toward the house. "I built the cabin where we ate breakfast first. The spring was running out of the bluff just below the cabin." He walked around the cabins and began telling how when they started having kids, they ran out of room. "I built the next cabin just across the hall."

It was an interesting story, and it covered a period of less than 20 years. Mr. Morrow never told Carl how many children he had. There were obviously two families in the room where they ate breakfast. The men ate at the table where Carl ate his breakfast. He had been too busy in conversation to try to figure out who was who.

"Son, I would invite you to stay here, but we're crowded already," Mr. Morrow concluded the conversation as they walked back toward the barn. Carl had hung his backpack on one of the hangers in the barn. He took it down and began putting it on when Mr. Morrow said to. "Go up the creek. Check everybody out, starting with the farm just south of here. If you don't find a place to stay, when you get to the Sitton place at the bridge, Willie will hire you." Carl walked away, pleased with the morning he had spent at the Morrow Place.

# CHAPTER 5

Following the logging trails along the edge of the bluff was better than pulling his shoes off to wade the creek every hundred yards. The first farmstead he came to after leaving the Morrow place was occupied by the Reece family. During the conversation about their place and where Carl had lived on the west side of Big Creek, he had learned that the farm used to be the Blair Homestead. When he asked if it was the place where the Jayhawkers killed the folks, the answer was yes. That was one of the first stories he remembered hearing as a boy. The way the story went they were shot after they had given everything they owned to the Jayhawkers. After showing Carl around the yard and the area where the Blair family was shot, Mr. Reece pointed to the hollow to the north.

"That's the mouth of the Bratton," pausing before he went on to say, "it's where everybody says Willie Sitton has a moonshine still."

The conversation continued with a description by Mr.

Reece of all the things Willie Sitton was involved in. There was no need to ask for work. There were several young boys, older than Carl, who sat several yards away and never took part in the conversation. He left their yard and followed the trail to the creek bank where Bratton Creek joined Big Creek. There was a well-traveled wagon road going south from the mouth of the Bratton. Carl wondered if Willie Sitton made enough trips to the still for the road to be that well established. It was easy walking in the wagon wheel ruts.

Walking along the east side of the creek, He could see the farmsteads being developed on top of the hills. Mr. Morrow told him there was no need to look for work at the places being built on the ridges.

"There's no water close to some of those places," he said, going on to explain how much trouble it would be to try to dig a cistern to catch water when it rained or to carry it from the hollows up the hills.

Mr. Morrow concluded his opinion about the homesteads on the ridges by saying, "They can't survive".

Carl continued to follow the creek and wondered how far he was from the bridge.

The sun began to set. Once again, he decided to camp. As he unrolled his backpack to make his bed, he thought back to the people he had talked to at the farmsteads. They all said the same thing.

"Go see Willie Sitton. He always hires help but, he's hard to work for," they would say, pausing before adding, "because he works too hard."

Carl was tired and lonesome for the first time since he left the smoldering ashes of his home. He wished he had gone with his dad and sister. Sleeping on a gravel bar was uncomfortable. He was hungry. There had been a smell coming from his backpack all day. But he didn't check until he was unpacking to get his fishing line for catching a fish to roast for dinner.

For the last three hours, he had been extremely hungry. A pleasant surprise greeted him as he opened the backpack. How did they manage to put the food inside the main flap? There was a total of six biscuits, along with all the bacon and sausage wrapped in a cloth. He ate well. And, settled down for another night of sleeping on the gravel.

He awoke early. There was enough food left for his breakfast. He walked faster. Deciding he was not going to stop until He saw the bridge over Big Creek. He knew Willie Sitton's barn and blacksmith shop was at the end of the bridge.

It was midafternoon. His pace became faster as the bridge over Big Creek came into sight. The sunshine was bright, and he picked up the pace, anxious to meet Willie Sitton.

As he got closer, he could hear the clanging of a hammer striking an anvil. The sound became louder the closer he got. Carl wondered how to approach Willie Sitton. His reputation was well-known. He was an expert craftsman at sharpening tools and making the three-prong gig for spearing fish. A moonshiner who never actually made the shine himself. Carl was remembering the day before, when Mr. Reece pointed to the foggy haze rising and said, "Willie Sitton's boys are cooking shine somewhere on top of the bluff." He had pointed to a ledge just below where Bratton Creek joined Big Creek. "A lot of people know it's there," he said, turning to walk back toward his house. "Everybody knows about it, but no one is going to ever complain".

Carl's heart raced as he climbed the creek bank and began the walk across the bridge. The cables carrying the planks for the floor swayed with his steps. While the walk was a short one, it seemed to take forever before he reached the end of the bridge. Willie had not looked up from his work. He stuck whatever he was working on back into the forge to reheat just as Carl came to the gate in front of the blacksmith shop. Willie noticed Carl for the first time and waved him into the blacksmith shop without saying a word.

Willie was cranking the bellows extra fast. Carl pulled his backpack off and hung it on the gate post. He turned and walked into the shop, then he stood and watched Willie until he looked up and pointed to a block of wood for Carl to sit on. Willie didn't say a word while he was pulling the hot piece of metal from the forge. He was pounding the metal with the hammer to create an edge for a plow. Carl watched as he turned the metal each time before he struck it.

Willie didn't speak until he stuck the plow point in the water to temper it. The sizzling of the hot metal and the steam coming out of the water caught Carl's attention. He had been in blacksmith shops before, but he couldn't remember seeing the steam coming out of the water.

"Where are you headin'?" Willie asked.

Carl didn't know how to respond. Before he decided on an answer, Willie continued. "You're that Harris boy, that's been coming up the creek for almost a week now. One of Cal Morrow's boys told me about you yesterday," Willie said as he removed the plow point from the water.

During the time Willie was tempering the plow point and laying it on the table with the rest of the finished tools, Carl still hadn't answered, nor introduced himself or responded to any of Willie's comments. He was observing Willie. Carl was five feet, eight inches tall, and he believed he might be taller than Willie., but the similarity of their bodies ended with their height. Carl had muscular shoulders and heavy hands developed from hard work, even though he was only fourteen years old. Willie was the same size from head to toe. His hands appeared small, but it was because his forearms were extremely large from working in the blacksmith shop.

Neither one of them was conscious of the time they spent observing each other. Willie finally broke the silence. "They tell you I might let you work?"

Carl finally broke his silence. "Yes, everybody told me you always hired help."

"What would I need you to do?" Willie smiled for the first time. He had not shown any facial expressions since Carl stepped into the shop.

"I don't have any idea, Mr. Sitton," he stammered.

Before he could continue, Willie interrupted. "Don't call me 'Mister'" he said sternly, and then smiled. "I'm Willie."

Carl stuck out his hand. "I'm Carl Harris."

They shook hands. Willie looked at Carl's hand when he turned it loose. He felt the strength of the handshake and he wondered how a young boy could have heavy calluses on his hands. As he summed up Carl further, he liked him.

Carl had made the same observation after the handshake. The calluses in Willie's hand and the strength of the handshake were different than any man Carl ever shook hands with before. When he thought about it, he had never shaken hands with over three or four men before. It was something only men did. The handshake meant Carl was a man looking for a job, not a boy looking for a handout. It was settled. Carl was going to work for Wille Sitton, the moonshiner.

Later that day, Carl was lying on the bed looking at the ceiling in the cabin. He had put his bed roll on top of the mattress. The mattress was on a bunk and there was a potbellied stove in the corner. Willie took him to the cabin and told him he would be back the next morning. There had not been any discussion about the work he would be doing.

Carl woke up early. It was not daylight. He didn't have a plan. He wondered what time Willie would be arriving. He dressed and washed his face in the old washbasin that was turned upside down on the shelf behind the back door of the cabin. He got water from a small stream. He knew it was a Spring Branch flowing behind the cabin. He was just walking back to the front of the cabin when he saw Willie coming with a wagon pulled by two mules.

The wagon barely stopped before Willie said, "Get on the wagon."

Willie gave the order before he greeted him with a friendly good morning.

He turned the wagon around before Carl sat down well on the seat. He handed the reins to Carl. "You ever drive a wagon?"

Carl was going to answer, "no", but as he got the mules under control, he answered, "I have now." They both laughed.

During the wagon ride, they began a conversation about what Willie wanted Carl to do. Without asking any questions about his background, he began telling Carl about his three girls and said he needed a young man, a boy to help him with all his chores.

"If you can do everything, I need you to do…" Willie paused. "…I can keep you busy just running errands and doing the things I don't have time to do."

The next hour was spent touring the farm and feeding different herds of livestock. Willie would point the direction he wanted Carl to go in without interrupting his stories about the farm. He didn't tell Carl that they were going back to his house for breakfast until they were stopped in the front yard.

Without saying a word, Willie got off the wagon and started into the house, only stopping long enough to tie the mules to the hitching post. Carl followed him, not knowing what was next.

"Ellen, we have to feed this boy," Willie said as they passed through the back room where the table was covered with food. "This is Carl Harris, the boy from down the creek."

It was all the introduction Carl got to Willie's wife, Ellen. He followed Willie to the back porch and washed his hands, getting ready to eat breakfast. When they were seated at the table, Ellen introduced him to their daughters. He was seated at one end of the table, and Willie was at the other end. Ellen sat to his left, and one of the older girls was on the same side as her. The youngest girl was seated next to Carl, facing her mother, and the third girl was sitting beside her.

"This is Carl Harris." Ellen began a complete introduction. "He is the man your dad told us about last night."

Carl looked at Ellen when she called him a man. It was the first time he had been referred to like that. He still considered himself a boy. During the course of the meal, Carl answered questions, with most of them being asked by the youngest daughter. He learned her name was Pauline and she had just turned twelve years old. When he looked at the other two girls, they didn't smile. They were friendly in conversation, but they did not seem pleased to have him eating at their table. Pauline was a different story. Every time Carl looked at her, she would smile and seemed to be staring when he would look away.

The food was different than what he was used to. There were the usual biscuits and gravy everybody served for breakfast, but there was also fried chicken. Carl couldn't remember eating fried chicken for breakfast, except once in Mississippi when his grandmother cooked for the whole family. He couldn't remember how many people were gathered for the Harris reunion before they left Mississippi.

There was quite a time lapse while they were eating breakfast. Willie didn't seem to be in a hurry, and he was quiet most of the time while Ellen asked Carl questions. Pauline, the youngest daughter, continued to show interest in Carl and was shocked when he told Mrs. Sitton that he was just fourteen years old.

He felt her staring at him after he told her his age. He had shaved a few times the year he turned twelve. Since then, his beard had grown full and thick, too much for a fourteen-year-old boy. He kept it trimmed and neat, a lot neater than his hair had been for the last couple of months.

Pauline—Carl remembered her name but had no idea about the names of the two older girls—had said, "I like his hair and beard."

"Pauline!" Her mother said with a tone meant to scold her.

Willie joined the conversation for the first time. "Pauline always says whatever comes in her mind."

Everybody laughed, including Carl, and Pauline's face turned red as she looked at her dad.

The meal ended on a good note. Willie followed Carl back to the wagon.

He knew his life had just made a big change. He had no idea where his relationship with Willie Sitton was heading and could not anticipate what was next.

# CHAPTER 6

Carl was back in the cabin after spending the day with Willie. It had been a good day, starting with driving the wagon and visiting with Willie before joining Mrs. Sitton and their daughters for breakfast. The food was great. Ellen Sitton had cooked the best food he had ever eaten. Plus, he got to meet the three girls. He was especially smitten by Pauline and the attention she gave to him.

When he got back to the cabin, he barely recognized it. It smelled clean. He first thought that someone had taken his backpack, but he located it sitting in the corner behind the wood stove. He quickly made note of the double lace knot he used to tie the backpack together. His dad had taught him how to tie the knot.

"Son, you will have no need to worry about anyone getting into your stuff if you use this knot," he had told him. "You will know it if they do."

Carl remembered how long it took for him to learn to tie the knot by weaving the laces together. He never saw anyone outside the Harris family who knew how to tie the knot on his backpack. It was secure.

There was a bucket of water sitting on the shelf with a long handled galvanized dipper hanging off the side. There was also a towel hanging above the washbasin. He had noticed the nail for the towel the day before, when he washed his face. Everything was spotless. He wondered who put in the effort to clean the cabin and why.

His biggest surprise came when he went to bed. A clean quilt covered the full length of it. When he folded it back, there was a pillow covered by a pillowcase with fancy trim. who?

The new quarters were pleasing but he didn't understand why he was being treated so well. The first night was spent on a mattress with no bedding or springs. There was now a pad supported by suspension springs. The bed was the best one Carl ever had. There were three pots hanging by their handles in the corner above the backpack. He wondered if he was expected to start preparing his own food. Cooking with a stove would be a new experience However, he was very adept at cooking over a campfire.

The cabin was more than he ever dreamed about having when he walked away from the fire burning his home. Before he went to sleep, he tried to remember all the things he had done. Willie had talked continuously as they went to different fields along the creek. They fed steers somewhere up the creek from the cabin. They had gone up the mountain across from the cabin to check a cornfield. The sharecropper was not there, and the field looked unattended. Carl had seen Willie's temper for the first time.

"This field needs cleaned off and the ground broke, now," Willie said as they drove across the dry barren ground.

It only took a few minutes for Willie to begin talking again. Carl listened. After dinner before he returned to the cabin, they had gone for a tour of the work Willie's grandfather did when the Sitton place was settled by the

Sitton family. He had listened as Willie explained how the flow of the spring behind the Sitton Homestead was changed by his great uncle Eric Huckabee and his grandfather Noah.

"It was all Granddad's idea, but without Uncle Eric to do the blasting, the water would never be flowing like it is now," he said. They had followed the water as it flowed in and out of each corral. When they got to the last one, he saw that it was the deepest of the pools in the corrals.

"Be quiet. I want you to see the fish we keep here," Willie had spoken in a whisper. He took a huge net off the fence and showed Carl how he could dip up the fish swimming in the pool. He went on to explain, anytime they caught more than they wanted to fry they were dumped into the pool for later.

When Carl started walking 'home', the thought of home didn't settle in until he was climbing the hill toward the cabin. It would only be a week tomorrow since he left the smoldering embers where his mother and sister were buried.

For some reason, he felt secure. Willie Sitton made no promises, but he also made it clear it was special having Carl Harris along with him on the wagon seat all day. At each stop he went into details of what each farm and the farmer meant to the Sitton plan. Carl wondered about the moonshine still. Ever since his family arrived in the Cozy home community, they heard stories about Willie Sitton, the moonshiner.

Carl was not religious. His family came to Arkansas from the northeast corner of Mississippi. They lived on the Tennessee River in the mountains north of the river. They were just south of Wayne County Tennessee. While the Harris family never participated in making moonshine, there was always a jar of liquid available to make a toddy.

Carl went to sleep. The plan for the next day was for him to go to the barn, feed the stock and hitch up the mules to the wagon.

"We'll start our day when I get to the barn, Carl," Willie

said as Carl left the corral after seeing the fish in the pool of water. He observed the pride Willie expressed while showing him everything. He was anxious to see what was in store during his stay at the Sitton Homestead.

# CHAPTER 7

Carl Harris had left his homestead around the first of April 1925. On the last Saturday in June, he was sitting in the second row of pews, in the Cedar Creek schoolhouse. He was at the end of the pew next to the aisle. Willie was standing in the back, leaning against the wall. Ellen Sitton was helping conduct the meeting. It was a session to plan Fourth of July festivities and the start of a two-month session of school.

Willie insisted Carl attend the meeting. The first month he lived in the cabin, there had been a continuous flow of new shirts and other clothes brought to the cabin. The first time they took his laundry it was returned with two new shirts. They were a little larger than the old ones, they were a perfect fit.

He looked down at his new shoes. He had gone to Marshall with Willie, and they were shopping in a big general store for supplies. His shoes were well worn, and he was looking at the boots when Willie came by.

Willie picked up the boots and asked, "Will these fit you, Carl?"

When Carl shook his head, Willie asked him to try them on. They fit. Willie handed him a twenty-dollar bill and told him to go pay for them. When he returned, he offered the eight dollars in change to Willie.

"Son, keep that money," Willie said. "I need to start paying you a regular salary."

Carl's thoughts went back to the day he started working at the bridge. He still was not receiving regular pay. He had more clothes than ever before in his life. He really didn't understand his new situation. Every day from daylight to dark, he was a part of the Sitton family.

"Willie, Pauline is going crazy about that boy," Ellen Sitton said later. Carl overheard her. Pauline took advantage of any opportunity to follow him around, and Carl enjoyed it.

Ellen made sure her daughter and Carl never had an opportunity to be alone.

When they got to the schoolhouse, Ellen told Pauline, "You can sit with Carl."

Willie was shocked and smiled as he watched Carl and Pauline sit down next to each other in the pew. He was approving of their relationship.

Ellen was conducting the meeting.

"We are here to plan our fourth of July celebration and to discuss our next school term," she said nervously, without looking directly at Pauline or Carl.

She began the discussion about the school term by introducing the teachers. There were going to be two teachers: a woman teaching the children ten years old and under, and a man teaching the older kids. As Carl listened to the meeting, he remembered Willie asking how much schooling he had.

While trying to listen to the plans for school, Carl was lost in thoughts about how much he had gone to school and what he had told Willie.

He told Willie before they left Mississippi, he had attended three sessions. During three terms of school, he had learned to write, read, and do some arithmetic.

Willie had said, "I want you to go some this term." That was on Monday before the Saturday meeting. Carl thought no more about it until he was feeding the animals and Willie said, "We've got to hurry if we are going with Ellen and the girls to the schoolhouse."

Carl's life changed every day after the day he sat down in the blacksmith shop. His work had been a little bit of everything. He was told to take a load of corn to the mouth of Bratton. "Park the wagon and tie the mules to the tree next to the crossing," Willie continued. "Take your fishing pole; try to catch a few fish. Someone will come and get the wagon."

There was no explanation for why the corn was going to the whiskey still. He was not told who would come and get the wagon and was surprised when it was Willie's cousin. Carl had never met Nate Huckabee, but he understood he made the moonshine. He delivered the jars of 'shine Willie sold out of the barn.

It was never discussed with Carl, but after he made that first trip delivering corn, he brought back the 'shine to be sold in the barn. It became a regular trip every other week.

After the discussion with the teachers, they started making plans for the Fourth of July picnic. Carl's mind came back to the present, and he was listening to the plans for a picnic below the Cedar Creek schoolhouse at the Huckabee hole, where Bare Branch joined Big Creek. Different people volunteered to bring different food. Willie was roasting two pigs. Others began volunteering to do different things.

Nate Huckabee said, "I hope we can have watermelon, mine are close to getting ripe."

"I've got some that I know are ripe," Mr. Morrow said. It was the first time Carl noticed him sitting in the front left of the building. It was Carl's first meeting at the Cedar Grove school building. There were many people present he had never seen before.

Pauline began to whisper. "Are you going to swim?" she asked Carl. His face flushed red. He never swam for pleasure, though he had started swimming early, as a child in Mississippi. They swam when they noodled fish. Before moving to Arkansas, most of the fish in northeast Mississippi was harvested by noodling.

"No," Carl answered. He would not be swimming.

"Mama won't let us girls swim, either" Pauline said it loud enough everybody heard it. There was a ripple of laughter. Ellen Sitton came back but didn't ask what was funny. Willie smiled broadly but did not laugh.

When they started walking home from the meeting, Carl and Pauline walked in front of the family. There were probably twenty people walking together when they crossed the swinging bridge over Big Creek. The bridge swayed as the people walked across, and Pauline giggled. Carl and Pauline were having a good time. Maybe it was the date? Neither he nor Pauline had any idea what their relationship was, or how fast it was developing.

Willie Sitton had a plan. He was training Carl to become the son he never had, and a son-in-law. Carl went home to the cabin. His thoughts were more confused than ever before, but he was not lonesome. He was at home on Big Creek.

# CHAPTER 8

**A** slight chill was in the August air. Carl Harris laid the algebra book on the large cut of wood which served as a poker table in the barn. He went to school three days a week and studied two subjects. He remembered the conversation with Willie after the Fourth of July picnic. It was a big event. It was held in a field above the Huckabee hole and on the gravel bar.

School started the next Monday. Carl was embarrassed to go, but when he arrived, there were three men in their thirties trying to learn to read. Education was getting a new emphasis.

"I want you to learn as much as you can," Willie had said. He insisted Carl attend the school. When he laid the algebra book on the desk, he placed the last assignment on top. He walked to the barn with Pauline Sitton. Their relationship was growing. They held hands one day as they walked across the bridge and didn't see Willie leaning against the railing until they were immediately in front of him.

Pauline had jerked her hand away, but when Willie said, "Go ahead, Pauline. Hold his hand, I would be disappointed if you didn't."

That was the end of them being embarrassed. They would now hold hands as they walked anywhere. Carl's studies and his work kept him busy.

Willie joined Carl in solving the algebra problems. Carl did not understand Willie's fascination with mathematics. Willie seemed to enjoy learning more about the process of algebra.

"I like the logic of looking for the unknown," was a remark he constantly made when Carl handed him the problem of the day.

Farm work centered around checking all the sharecroppers and making sure they were tending to the fields. They made a trip every day to one of the farmsteads. It was a constant learning process for Carl. Willie seldom mentioned the moonshine business, but Carl continued to deliver corn to the crossing below the mouth of Bratton Creek. He always fished until the wagon was returned. He visited with Nate Huckabee, but never asked any questions about how to get up to the still.

Willie walked into the barn. He picked up the algebra lesson and didn't pick up the book.

"This is going to be a tough one; we have three brackets around two unknowns." Willie picked up the chalk and one slate and handed the other slate to Carl. The race was on. It had become a ritual for each one of them to work on their own and see who could solve the algebra problem first.

Carl usually finished first, but he learned early on to wait and let Willie win at least half the time. Neither one of them understood the significance of a middle-aged man and a teenage boy competing in math. Their relationship was developing. Was it a father-son relationship? Was it friendship? It lacked a description. The young man who decided to not leave Big Creek and go to Oklahoma with his dad and sister was happy. He only hoped to find a place to live. The older man knew he was missing something, too. He remembered the days when he was following his great uncle Eric Huckabee around. Since that time, there had always been a missing part of his life.

Willie had learned to listen during the trip to Colorado, when he had helped carve a marker for grave with his uncle Eric. He now wanted to teach Carl the same things he had learned from Eric Huckabee, like he had as soon as the Morrow boy told him about Carl leaving his home and walking up Big Creek for a week before he arrived at the barn. Maybe it was his attitude. Carl was always polite, but he was confident. Willie never saw fear in the young man. He liked the day he handed him the reins to drive the wagon. He could tell when he took them, he didn't know how to drive the mules. But by the time he answered, he had changed his grip on the reins until he was in control of the mules.

Since his arrival at the bridge, Carl Harris always seemed to have a knack for knowing what Willie wanted him to do next. Even Willie didn't know why he chose to work the algebra problems with Carl. Maybe he wanted to know more, or was it that he didn't want Carl learning more than he knew?

Willie Sitton always planned what his next move would be. He saw a way to carry his heritage forward through Carl Harris, a son he never expected to have.

# CHAPTER 9

**D**uring the summer school session, Carl and Willie's relationship continued to grow while they completed the study of algebra. Pots for cooking were still hanging on the wall behind the stove. They had never been taken down nor used. He was no longer a guest at the Sitton dinner table. He sat in the same chair every time. It was the same place where he sat the first time, when he ate with them. The only thing different now was that Pauline made a point of serving his food. She used the time to catch up on what Carl and Willie were doing. Ellen and Willie seldom interrupted her constant chatter and questions.

An after-dinner walk around the properties became their typical date during the summer. Harvest season was about to begin, and there wouldn't be as much time for them to spend together once it started.

The first part of the harvest was to strip the leaves from the sorghum cane. There was a covered area next to the barn where they were stored and fed to the steers. After the sorghum leaves were gone, a combination of hay and the heads of the sorghum cane was fed. Willie always switched the steers' feed to corn before they went to the meatpackers.

Carl stopped the wagon at the end of the sorghum rows. He was on the bench land above Big Creek. The land was the same as it was around the buildings at the Sitton Homestead. He was on the bluff a mile north of the barn. Willie was bringing another wagon to the same field. They were going to start stripping the leaves off the sorghum.

Willie explained. "We gotta get the leaves off before frost."

He went into considerable details about why the leaves had to be taken off early. An early frost would make the molasses "taste funny", a slightly bitter taste that got worse the longer the juice was cooked. Stripping the leaves and left the heads of grain on until the first frost protected the taste.

While Carl listened to the explanation, he did not have a clue what it meant. The Harris family never grew any sorghum cane for molasses. They bought honey and molasses from a couple of neighbors in Mississippi, and after settling in Arkansas they bought molasses made by Willie Sitton and the Morrow family.

He couldn't remember what farm chores they would be doing during molasses-making time. He didn't know why it was his first-time stripping leaves from sorghum cane. His job was to tie the leaves in bundles and load them into the wagon. He understood the cane stalks were going to be left standing after the leaves were stripped. Willie gave a lengthy description of the color of the grain in the head of the cane before they would cut it and make the molasses.

"The heads have to be ripe enough for the seeds to shatter before we cut the cane." He had pointed at the tops which were a deep yellow. "When they start showing some dark color it will be time to start making the molasses."

Carl had listened while Mr. Blair talked with Willie about how he enjoyed cooking the cane juice for the sorghum.

"If we cut the cane at the right time, we won't have much green foam to skim off when we start cooking," Newt Blair declared as they all stood, admiring the cane field.

There must have been twenty people gathering to start stripping the cane. There were five or six older women. Ellen Sitton arrived in the buggy with Pauline and her other two daughters. Carl had no idea this was going to be such a large effort by the entire community.

"I brought enough to eat for all of us," Ellen Sitton said to Willie as she pulled the buggy alongside the wagons.

Carl began to understand. Molasses time at Big Creek was an event.

The bundles of leaves in both wagons were piled high. He started to pull away and stopped, realizing he did not know where he was going with the bundles.

"Where are we taking these?" he asked Willie.

"To the little barn just below the house," Willie replied. "We feed 'em to the steers."

Carl knew where he was going. He did enjoy taking the bundles from Pauline as she tied them together and handed them to him. He still didn't see how they were able to tie so many leaves together with two leaves used for ties. They were solid enough he was able to take a hold of the tie and pitch them on to the wagon without them coming apart. He would check that out when he got to the little barn and started to unload. There had to be a knack to tying the leaves. He thought back to when he was taught to tie the lace knot he used on his backpack. Tying a knot was a skill. Each knot, regardless of where or how you were tying it, was different.

Carl remembered when he learned to tie the lace knot, thinking, *"whoever figured this out in the first place?"*

He rolled along in the wagon. He wanted to hurry and get unloaded and back to the field. The last thing he heard before he left the field was Ellen Sitton declaring that they would eat lunch as soon as they returned.

# CHAPTER 10

The first week in October after stripping the cane, Willie handed a tool for cutting the cane to Carl. It was a blade fastened at a square angle to a handle that was just over three feet long. He examined the blade. It was sharp on the upper side. Willie held the handle out.

"You reach past the cane stalk, and with a quick jerk, pull the knife through the stalk. We want to cut them as close to the ground as possible," Willie explained.

Carl was at a loss. He had never seen the tool before, and he had never cut a stalk of cane. There was a total of eight handles laying in the wagon, and Carl followed Willie and the other wagon back to the cane field next to the creek. He had listened intently while Mr. Blair and Willie discussed the type of sorghum each field of cane would produce. The field along the creek in the rich, dark soil would make stronger, richer molasses. The cane fields on the ridges would make lighter yellow, milder molasses. The sandy soil of the bench land would make the sweetest, which was

Willie's favorite.

Willie explained, "We are cutting the bottom land cane first because the seeds are shattering from the heads."

Supposedly that was the time when the molasses should be made. Carl had been with Willie twice in the same field when they cut a sample of the cane and sucked the juice to see if it was sweet enough. He had no idea what it was supposed to taste like.

"I can still taste a little bit of green," Willie said the first time after they tasted the juice from the cane. "We will start cutting tomorrow," he said the day before Carl met him in the barn where he was loading the knives—or whatever the contraptions were with the blades at the end of the handles.

They drove to the field above the barn. It was the richest bottom land on the Sitton Homestead. The stalks of cane were much taller than the ones they pulled the leaves from first. Carl hated it when they were stripping the leaves because he had to bend the stalks over to reach the top leaves. They left their heads intact. While they were standing, discussing where to start, people began showing up to cut cane.

As usual, Ellen Sitton showed up with the girls ready to help. Pauline immediately looked for her favorite cutting knife.

"This is it," she said, taking the handle away from Carl. He thought she was kidding. He had been struggling with how to use the knife. He stood in amazement as Pauline was grabbing stalks of cane and snipping them off just above the ground with the pull knife.

"This is the third year I've been allowed to cut cane," she told Carl with a smile.

He began picking up the stalks as she cut them and removing the heads of grain. They were standing the cane in shocks leaned together like a teepee. There was an art to getting started with the shock of cane. Two people leaned the cane they had in each hand together and held it while other people added a couple more to the start of the shock. Carl learned to do it quickly. He didn't ask why it was called a shock. He was learning the harvest of cane and enjoying it.

When the wagon was full of heads, Willie told Carl, "Take these to the same barn you put the leaves in. The seeds that shattered out in the wagon, sweep them up and put them in a sack. They are the seed for next year's crop."

He learned later that the seeds that shattered were the most mature of any in the head. The first seeds to ripen had a harder shell and would stay dry during the winter and germinate quicker when planted. He could not believe the excitement of the people coming to work on the cane. All the talk was about making molasses.

The day finally came. Carl was told to haul as much cane as he could to the sorghum mill. He passed the press for squeezing the juice from the stalks several times. Willie told him all summer that it would be an exciting place come molasses time. When he arrived with the first load of cane, there were two wagons hauling wood to fire the pan and to cook the juice. The pole to turn the rollers of the sorghum mill was fastened in place. The two mules that took turns turning the mill were there ready to start.

Carl unloaded in the spot Willie showed him and left for another load. He met a wagon hauling a load of cane driven by a young man he had never seen before. It seemed to him every neighbor was showing up to help with the molasses.

When Carl returned with the second load, he recognized preacher Ed Tice talking to Willie.

He heard the preacher ask Willie who he was.

Although he had seen the preacher a couple of times at Cozy, he never had met him.

He remembered hearing the gossip around the time his mother died of how the preacher was drinking with Willie Sitton. Carl never went to church. The Harris family was not religious. Although he had stood quietly after his mother was buried, the only people present were his dad and his sister.

There were no prayers. There were not any songs. Now he wished he had gone for preacher Ed to say something at her grave.

Willie introduced him. "This is Carl Harris. He has been working all summer. He lives in the cabin." Willie pointed toward the house Carl was staying in.

There was no other explanation. After a few minutes he heard Willie tell Preacher Ed, "Come on with me, we'll haul cane."

He started toward Carl's wagon and told Carl to help with the fire. Carl lost his job of hauling cane to the preacher and Willie. He began selecting the wood and placing it inside the area where the pan for cooking the juice was being set. Ellen Sitton and the girls showed up. Newt Blair was going to cook the juice.

The mules were walking in a circle, and the cane was piled close to the press, out of their path. The juice was running into a tank just above the pan. The fire was burning brightly. There was no smoke; it was good, dry wood.

Newt Blair was scrubbing the pan, making sure it was clean. It was ready. He opened the spicket and the juice flowed into the pan. He let it flow until it covered the entire bottom. The steam began to rise, and he ladled it back, away from the finish area. He was ladling it until it started to boil. Carl watched as he used the baffles to push the juice back and forth as it cooked. He watched him skim off the green foam forming as the juice started to boil.

Carl went back to work carrying more cane to the press. He was told by someone he had never seen before, "We need pitchforks to handle the pummies."

Carl had no idea what the pummies were. Someone had to explain to him that it was the name of cane after the juice was squeezed out.

After a trip to the barn and he returned with three pitchforks. The Huckabee family arrived with jars for the molasses.

There was an unbelievable amount of work involved in making molasses. The Harris family never tried to make molasses. He only hoped it was worth the effort.

He had been too busy to even notice Pauline when she started unloading the jars and setting up the racks for keeping the molasses. The hot molasses had to be placed on shelves to cool.

The sun was beginning to set, and there were several jars of molasses sitting full on the rack.

"Cal Morrow made sixty quarts on Wednesday," Willie said when he and the preacher had made it back with a load of cane and gave the report of how well the neighbor was doing. He concluded by saying, "We will make more than that tomorrow."

# CHAPTER 11

The October sunset was accented by the golden clouds. The smoke from the molasses being cooked was drifting slowly down toward the creek. It was going to be a cold night. There was scattered frost several mornings while they were harvesting the cane. It was warm in the cabin when Carl got back the first day it turned cold outside. Someone had built a fire for him, and there was additional wood stacked on the little porch in front of the cabin.

"Probably Pauline built this fire," he whispered under his breath. Since coming to the Sitton place, he had learned the girls could do everything around the farm. That was the last thought he had before he entered the cabin.

Carl heard Willie several times say, "We got the cane stripped just in time." Then he would continue by saying, "A little frost never hurts the cane after it is stripped. It actually makes it sweeter."

Carl watched the pan as Willie was working the last of the molasses. He was moving them toward the section where they would be finished and drained into jars. They were a bright golden color. The cane came from the first ledge where they stripped the leaves. Carl heard continuously how the light sand and gravel mixed soil grew the best cane and the sweetest flavored molasses. He was tired of eating the foam and samples from the last two days of cooking, but when he tried a small sample of the batch just being finished, he understood why everybody wanted the sweet molasses. Pauline filled the last of the jars with the good-flavored molasses. They were too hot to carry and put in the buggy.

Willie gave one jar to Preacher Ed. He put it in a 'tow' sack and the preacher tied it on to the back of his saddle. He was riding a little red mule. Carl had heard about the preacher riding a mule too small for him. When he rode away, everyone watched. Carl wondered what was going through the people's minds. He had joined the preacher and Willie in their conversations the last few days. The preacher was showing up every morning after they started making molasses.

You could say the same thing about everyone in a five-mile radius. He had met more people in the last few days than ever before in his life. Everybody seemed to know who he was. He wore the boots, and the shirts Willie and Ellen provided him with after he arrived at the Sitton Homestead. He didn't notice that his shirts were identical to Willie's until one of the Huckabee boys mentioned that Aunt Ellen "made that shirt of yours".

He was proud. While he didn't understand everything about his new relationship with Willie and his family, Carl felt at ease. Willie made it clear to everybody that he was there to stay. He heard him tell Preacher Ed, "I am going to teach that boy everything he needs to know about running this place."

As Carl walked away, he heard the preacher ask Willie, "Does that include how to make moonshine?" They laughed after the preacher asked the question."

There were no more stalks of cane waiting for the juice to be squeezed out of them. The pile of pummies was huge. Carl wasn't sure what would become of them. He had gathered all the shattered seeds from the wagon beds after hauling the heads to the barn. The seed was in sacks, and Willie tied them up and they were hanging in the hallway of the little barn next to the house. It was the second barn Noah Sitton built after he settled on the ledge.

In the six months Carl had been living at the Sitton Homestead, he learned the history behind every building. Including when the big barn was built at the end of the bridge. Willie built that barn to house his moonshine business. He sharpened tools in the blacksmith shop. He sold moonshine out of the room with the big block of wood and the six stools around it. He never explained to Carl what they were used for.

Carl found out their use when he was sent on an errand up the creek and returned early. There was a collection of horses and buggies sitting next to the barn but there was no one outside. Carl opened the door, and there were cards and money on the big block with men sitting on all the stools. A card game was in progress. He realized the rumors about the games were true. It was the first time he saw one firsthand. He closed the door and went back to his wagon and began unhitching the mules.

After he was finished feeding the mules and brushing them down with the curry comb, the game was finished, and Willie came to check on him.

"Don't you ever play a game of poker," Willie said matter-of-factly. "I've played for years, but it's not a good thing."

Willie turned and walked away from Carl and did not give any further explanation. Carl never asked him any questions about anything he said. All the things Carl ever heard about cards being played in the barn were not good things. There were times when he questioned whether his mother would be happy with his new lifestyle. Carl would not be asking Willie any further questions about the games or the moonshine.

# CHAPTER 12

Fall was always one of Carl's favorite times. All the crops were harvested and most of the work being done was taking care of the animals. Willie was re-working the hog pens and trying to decide how many hogs he wanted to keep for breeding purposes and how many he planned to fatten for slaughter. He was standing next to an empty pen when Carl approached him.

"Do you think you could catch some of those pigs your daddy turned loose?" Willie asked Carl. The question surprised Carl. He didn't know what Willie had in mind.

"I don't have any idea which direction they went after dad tore down the pen," he answered.

"Fred Hudson said he saw four of the pigs running along the West Bank of Buffalo River just above the mouth of Big Creek."

Willie had more information than Carl realized.

"You're talking about the white hogs that Dad brought from Mississippi? He got them at the same time he brought back the red pole heifers." Carl thought he knew the pigs Willie was referring to.

"Yeah, that's them," Willie said as he sat down on the back of the wagon. They had finished hauling the pummies and the rest of the trash from the area of the molasses mill. They took the pan after Ellen cleaned it enough to suit her before it was stored and hung it upside down in the loft of the big barn. Willie insisted it had to be hung upside down to keep the birds and anything else from nesting in the pan before it was used again.

They left the hog pen and stopped in front of the barn. The conversation continued before they unhitched the mules.

"You want to go down there to the Buffalo River and see if you can locate three or four of the pigs?" Willie said as Carl joined him and sat down in the wagon.

"I guess." He hesitated before he went ahead and said, "I could try."

Their conversation turned into a plan. Carl would take the wagon, along with some wire for a pen and some corn to try to catch some of the pigs. Willie suggested he take several lengths of rope to use for securing them while he brought them home.

"If you find them, try to bait them with corn," Willie added. "If you can get them to start eating the corn, they will follow it without realizing they are going into the pen." He was standing in front of Carl as he gestured with his hands like he was throwing corn on the ground. "Did you ever feed those pigs when you were at home?" he asked.

"I did it all," Carl answered. He did not like the discussion. The last year before his mother died had been exceptionally tough. His dad was responsible for taking care of her, and Carl took care of everything else. He had fed pigs. He had milked the cow. He took the grain to be ground for cornmeal. He did all the work until his mother was buried.

"Those pigs might know you" Willie said. Willie's hogs all recognized his voice, and he could call them back to their pen if they got out. He told Carl hogs had a better sense of smell and could recognize voices better than any other animal. Carl had never heard such a thing before. The plan was in place, Carl would go the next morning to try to find the pigs.

The sky to the east above the bridge was showing signs of the sun coming up when Carl met Willie at the barn. He was ready to make the trip to the mouth of Big Creek to try to locate some of the pigs his dad had turned loose before he left for Oklahoma. As he left the barn, he didn't drive the wagon across the bridge. Because he liked to drive the wagon through water, he went down the bank below the bridge and crossed the creek into the field.

The sound of the wagon wheels as they entered the water to cross Big Creek changed from the crunching of the gravel to the splashing sound of the spokes cutting through the water. The mule's steps were muffled by the water and the sound coming from their feet splashing was close to the same sound being made by the wheels.

Carl looked at the leaves on the trees. While they were not large enough to make a shadow in the spring when he started up the creek looking for work, they were now a brilliant color and steadily falling into the creek. It seemed like a lifetime since he woke up cold and confused in his yard that morning, before he left the burning house. He still didn't know why he chose to camp in the yard after he got to the fire.

Now he was returning to the place he left behind in the spring. A lot had changed since that day, today he was driving a wagon pulled by one of the best teams in the area. Also, he was living in a cabin and eating most of his meals with Willie and Ellen with a regular seat at the table. The seat on his left was where Pauline sat. Carl didn't really have a perspective of how much change had occurred since he walked for several days before he made it to the bridge and met Willie Sitton.

Who was he now? Carl didn't have any idea what lay in store for him. There was no way to predict how he would've been able to become a part of the Sitton family.

His sense of values was instilled by his mother. While they were not religious, they lived by a code. Mind your own business. Work hard. Stay clean. And respect your neighbor. Carl was bitter when he thought about all the things which destroyed his family. His mother's illness, his dad losing interest after the heifers were stolen.

Carl thought about having to go by Coy Bryant's barn. There was no other way to get to the place where the hogs were turned loose. There were a lot of thoughts going through his mind as he continually crossed the creek while heading north. It was exciting being able to ride across places— where he waded barefoot six months earlier—and to think he had the security of working for Willie Sitton. He was learning a lot of things, including a new set of values. Although he just met preacher Ed Tice, he could see where he was learning things that were a combination of what Willie Sitton and the preacher believed. He could see the compromises preacher Ed made trying to become Willie's friend. He also realized Willie's values were not being adjusted to accommodate preacher Ed. He liked the steadfastness of Willie's attitude, but he also like the sincerity he could feel in the new friendship with preacher Ed.

# CHAPTER 13

It had been over three hours since Carl left the bridge and was crossing the creek above Coy Bryant's barn. He was looking at the barn as he crossed the creek and remembered when he was told to stay away from it.

After they found their heifers standing in the corral, his dad said, "We have to fight the temptation to burn that barn."

The memories were fresh in Carl's mind as he listened to the wagon wheels throwing the water off as they came out of the creek. There was enough water flying from the wheels to almost get him wet as he got close to the barn. His thoughts were interrupted by a shotgun blast from inside the barn, and it scared the mules. The mules turned the wagon around and ran back toward the creek. A second shotgun blast caused them to run even faster. Carl got them under control and drove back to the barn and stopped about where he was when this first shotgun blast scared the mules.

After he got stopped, he went into the hallway of the barn.

He heard someone moaning. The sound was coming from the loft. He climbed the ladder and saw two people lying in the loft. The two bodies were practically nude, and both were bleeding profusely. He did not climb any higher, but stared at the bodies until he was sure they were dead. He was leaning toward them on his left hand extended on the loft floor but was still holding onto the ladder with one hand. He backed down the ladder and went back to the wagon.

He remembered passing the Hollimans where they were fishing. He turned the wagon around and crossed the creek, as he headed back to where he saw the Hollimans.

As soon as he got in sight of them, he started yelling, "There's been a killing!" He didn't remember what else he told the Holliman boys.

"I'll go back to the barn and wait," he believed he said as one of the boys joined him on the wagon. The other two dropped their fishing poles and started up the creek to get folks.

In the short period of time since the shotgun blast, a crowd had gathered. Carl knew how fast word could spread through the hills. When anyone went to a homestead and reported a problem, a runner was sent to the next homestead with the report while the rest of the people came to see if they could help. It was how people gathered when a house was burning or there was an accident. Today it was to investigate a shooting.

Carl was standing by his wagon where he had told the story several times. The last time he told it to Sheriff Joe Carson.

"After crossing the creek there was the first shotgun blast. The mules were spooked and ran back toward the creek, and it took a minute to gain control of them. It was sometime while I was gaining control of the wagon when I heard the second blast. There was the sound of a rider and I got a glimpse of the horse and the rider going over the hill into the cornfield. After tying the mules to the hitching post, I climbed the ladder into the loft. My head was just above the loft floor when I saw the woman. Taking a quick glance at the man I leaned out into the loft on one hand to get a closer look before I climbed back down the ladder. I went up the creek where I had passed the Holliman boys fishing. One of them came back with me while the rest of these people have come since the Hollimans spread the word. "There's been a murder in Coy Bryant's barn."

When the day was over, Carl drove the wagon to Marshall with Coy Bryant and Sister Rhodes' bodies wrapped in tarps. The county coroner took charge of the bodies. The day, filled with mystery, was over, and the crowd had to go home without answers. Two people had been shot in the loft of Coy Bryant's barn. Stories begin to spread with details unseen by Carl Harris and the witnesses at the scene.

# CHAPTER 14

Carl stood on the flat rock extending out into the creek. The rock was in the upper end of the swimming hole at the Big Creek bridge. He watched the water flowing out to the shoal and rapids before going underneath the bridge. A lot of things had changed in the past three years since the day of the shooting.

The murders continued to be the number one topic of discussion. As the day faded into his memory, Carl didn't remember when he went back to try to locate the pigs. He did find them and returned to the Sitton Homestead with a sow and four pigs. Willie was successful at cross breeding the white land Shire hogs with the black Duroc. There were now a good number of listed pigs. The hogs were born with a white strip circling their body just behind their shoulders. The Sitton farm was proud of the new breed. Willie bragged continuously every time a litter was born how much he appreciated Carl catching the hogs.

A lot of things were still changing. Carl was walking

toward the cabin where he lived when he first arrived at the farm. He was not living in the cabin alone. Pauline was now his wife. While the day of the shootings was over three years ago, he still had never discussed that day with Pauline. There was nothing about the shooter or the two people killed that interested Carl enough to want to have a discussion, but he had continually answered the same questions. He was trying to move on.

His marriage to Pauline was a foregone conclusion from the time he arrived at the Sitton Homestead until the day they were married. Romance? Carl was too busy to notice when his relationship with his wife changed from friendship to romance. It probably began the first time he shared a meal with the family. It went from holding hands while walking home from church and school functions to sitting on the edge of the bluff and watching the sunset.

They would go out after supper and watch darkness creep into the hollow. They enjoyed watching the shadows grow darker and the sounds of the night on Big Creek. One night an owl screeched, and Pauline grabbed him out of fear. They started with a hug, and before it was over, they were kissing and holding each other.

As they walked home, she suggested, "It might be time for us to tie the knot."

There was no more discussion. Carl told Willie, and he broke the news to Preacher Ed by saying, "There's a job for you the next time you're over this way."

Carl and Pauline went to the courthouse and got the marriage license on Thursday and were married the following Saturday underneath the shed covering the blacksmith shop. They were there with Preacher Ed, her parents, and the buggy with a horse hooked to it. They took the buggy and crossed Big Creek to the cabin.

Carl still wondered why Willie hooked up the buggy for him and Pauline to ride to the cabin. He took the buggy and horse back to the barn and walked home by himself later that night. Willie's gesture of harnessing the horse to the buggy was probably to watch them start their new life as they rode away. It was a special day at the Sitton Homestead.

Carl's attempt to put the discussions about the day at the barn out of his mind failed. Every discussion he heard about the shooting brought back the memories. The clearest of the memories was the blood dripping from the loft into the hallway of the barn as he walked in, stepping around it to climb the ladder before looking toward the front of the barn and the big open window of the loft. He barely got his head above the loft floor before he saw them. He saw Sister Rhodes with her head leaning against a post in the center of the loft. He remembered how her eyes were wide open and she seemed to be staring at the blood on her boobs.

He remembered seeing Coy Bryant lying face-down with his left arm extended out beside his head. His face was hidden like he was staring into his armpit.

The Holliman boys climbed the ladder and looked in the loft just like Carl had done earlier. He did not go back and look again. Carl stood in the hallway and talked to people as they arrived. He couldn't remember anybody going up where the bodies were until Sheriff Joe Carson and his deputies arrived.

He continued to think of all the stories about the scene in the barn until he was at the cabin door. When he entered the room, he was greeted by the smell of cornbread baking and the potatoes frying on the stove. Life was good, and Pauline could cook.

# CHAPTER 15

Carl stepped on the steppingstones just above the shoal. The stones were huge. They stayed above the water after the creek flushed up following a rain. A flood would cover them. Willie placed the stones there to keep the "kids" from having to wade the creek. Carl watched as the stones were placed in the creek. It was difficult to get them across the gravel bar. While the stones were being placed, Willie told the story of how he and his uncle Eric Huckabee moved a rock to mark a grave. It was where the Jayhawker was buried. When they finished the carvings, the mules pulled the marker into place.

Carl passed the stone his first trip up the creek. The story of Eric Huckabee carving a headstone because he was feeling guilty was only part of the story. While he felt bad about shooting the young man, the mystery of who he was and why he was carrying so much money bothered Eric. He kept the money for years and eventually returned it to the young man's family in Colorado. Willie would tell the story often. It was one of Carl's favorite stories.

Carl was learning the values Willie Sitton's family lived by. He was careful about making sure he was accurate when he told Willie anything. He learned to listen. He never interrupted anyone to correct them. He listened to people talk about the bodies of Coy Bryant and Sister Rhodes. They had descriptions that included things he knew were untrue. Willie told him to clean and oil the harness in the side room one afternoon soon after the shooting.

He was getting started cleaning the straps for the harness when Seth Tabor arrived at the shop. He never interrupted Willie when he was with someone. He listened as Willie and Seth went into the barn. He heard Willie when he was throwing cobs for a fire into the little stove. He knew he was going to make them a toddy.

He didn't hear Preacher Ed when he joined them, but then he heard every word of the discussion. It lasted for over an hour. Carl felt guilty. While he had continued to rub oil on the harness, he was quiet, listening to their discussion of the shooting.

He listened to the theory of the shooter hiding his horse inside the back stable. He listened to the theory that he had waited in the loft. He thought what Preacher Ed and Willie were really trying to do was to see if what they had heard would cause Seth Tabor to open up about what he had seen from the bluff. They knew he had spent the day on the west side of Big Creek. He was in a perfect spot, overlooking the field and the barn to see everything.

Seth never added anything to the conversation while Carl was listening.

Carl had been questioned so many times about the horse and rider. He could not remember nor add anything to the description. A glimpse of the horse as it disappeared over the hill was all he had seen. While he was listening to Willie and preacher Ed, he understood Seth Tabor had watched the horse riding toward him. He wondered about the description Seth could give.

He never planned to have any discussion with Seth Tabor. As far as Carl was concerned, he was ready to forget the day the shooting occurred. Carl's thoughts of things past ended.

# CHAPTER 16

The farm work had become routine. While Willie and Carl always spent a lot of time together, Carl's job was mostly tending to the livestock. He was supposed to manage the sharecroppers, making sure the fields were plowed and weed-free. A typical day would begin with him walking to the barn at the end of the bridge. He would hitch the mules to one of the wagons and load enough hay to feed the steers kept in the fields along the creek. After feeding the hay, he would take grain with salt mix to the cows and other stock being kept in the hillside pastures. Willie still fed the hogs in the pen close to the house. He was able to feed them from the top of the bluff. It was part of the enclosure and provided shelter for the hogs. It did not bother Carl that Willie wanted to feed the hogs. He hated the smell.

Carl's life had become more successful than he ever expected. When he walked away from the house fire, he was just hoping to survive. Willie gave him a job and it turned into an opportunity to become part of a family. Everyone recognized him as part of Willie Sitton's family.

A common remark was, "You're that boy of Willie's, the one he adopted to marry his daughter."

The comment never bothered Carl. The honesty and openness of Willie created a feeling of security. He was receiving all the benefits of being Willie Sitton's son, but he was still his own man. What other people thought could not damage the relationship between Willie and Carl.

The marriage worked out well with Pauline. She was becoming a good cook and housekeeper. It was exciting for Carl to wake up to the smell of bacon frying and biscuits in the oven. The cabin had been expanded with a new kitchen and dining area. They also had a separate bedroom from the original cabin area. The cabin where Carl was living when they were married had turned into a full-blown house. The front porch and steps had been expanded with a railing around it and steps at three different places.

It was a morning with bright sunshine as Carl walked to the barn. When he got there, Willie was loading bags of sugar, wheat shorts and some corn into the wagon. It was the first time Carl had seen a mixture of several different things being hauled in one load. He usually took a load of sugar or corn by themselves. He wondered why this load was a combination of several things. Were they going to mix the mash? It was always rumored how special and secret the recipe for the "Sitton moonshine" was.

"We're going to the still," Willie said.

Carl wondered if he was going to get his first trip to the Sitton whiskey still. While he had driven the wagon to the crossing several times, he had never gone around and up the hill to the still. He was sure the remark meant they were going to the still. Once again Carl's mind flashed back to his mother as he wondered what she would think of his new life and him being part of the moonshine business.

Willie was telling stories about all the things occurring during the years he had grown up at Big Creek. The splashing of the team and the noise of the wheels interrupted a story each time they crossed the creek. Willie had a story for every hole of water they passed in the creek. A memory of a catfish he killed with a two-pronged gig from underneath one of the rocks was a story Willie told every time they passed the rock. According to Willie, it was a big yellow catfish. While the fish were common in Buffalo River, it was unusual to see one in Big Creek.

Carl believed the fish got bigger every time Willie told the story.

"That thing must've weighed four pounds," Willie said the first time he told Carl about it. "That thing could've weighed five or six pounds," was the size of it today as the wagon passed the rock. Carl thought about how particular Willie was about making sure of the accuracy of a story.

*"The rules don't apply to a fish story,"* Carl thought, smiling as the wagon rolled along and Willie started a story about something else occurring while he was growing up along the creek. It was a good day and he wondered why he was going all the way to the still. The supplies were loaded in a particular order in the back of the wagon. He would learn why later in the morning.

# CHAPTER 17

The trough carrying the water to the barrels of mash could be moved to reach all of the barrels. The corn went in first, then they added the combination of oats and wheat mixed together to the corn. They were now filling the barrels with water. Each ingredient had been measured by Willie before he put them in the barrel.

"Don't ever breathe a word to anyone what we are putting in these barrels, or the order we put 'em in," Willie said very sternly, pointing at the barrels. "The mixture for good moonshine was discovered by the Sitton clan several generations ago," he added as he watched the water in each barrel rise to a mark and then moved it. None of the ingredients floated up to the top. Carl wondered why.

After the barrels filled to the proper level, Willie added dry wheat shorts which were ground extremely fine. The wheat shorts floated on top of the water. Willie measured out sugar and sprinkled it over the wheat shorts. He then retrieved a huge chunk of mash from a barrel sitting below the still. The mash was molded and looked spoiled to Carl.

"This is starter cake," Willie said as he dropped a chunk into the center of each barrel. He then stretched a cloth over the top of the barrel and tied it into place. He covered the barrels with corrugated roofing material and weighted it down with several large rocks.

"We will leave this alone for at least two weeks," Willie said as he loaded the leftover supplies into the wagon. There was no one else at the still. Willie showed Carl the thumper keg. "That's where we fire the mash, when it's ready to run." Willie pointed at top of the keg where a piece of copper pipe was connected "That curved copper pipe is called a worm. Don't ask me why."

There was no other explanation given about making moonshine. Carl drove the wagon back through the crevice off the bluff and up Bratton Creek. He turned down the creek and crossed the creek in the area where he always met the Huckabee's with corn and supplies.

He didn't know why Willie took him to the still and showed him how to mix the ingredients for the mash. He understood that Sitton moonshine was considered the best. He didn't ask if being shown the location of the still and how to mix the mash made him a part of the clan.

*"I am now Willie Sitton's son-in-law, and while it has privileges, it also has responsibilities,"* Carl thought. He knew it was a matter of trust for Willie to show him the route to the still. He also knew there was more trust involved in showing him how to mix the ingredients for making moonshine.

He wondered on the ride back to the bridge what Willie had in mind for him to do next. The conversation, as usual, was Willie telling stories about things that happened along the creek since they settled on the homestead almost one hundred years earlier.

# CHAPTER 18

Almost six weeks later, they returned to the still. The fire underneath the thumper keg had been burning for over an hour. Carl watched as Willie adjusted the pipe carrying smoke away from the fire into the crevice where the water flowed out of the hill. The smoke followed the crevice into the bluff. There was no smoke visible above it. Carl backed up away from the bluff to be able to see farther up the hill. It was amazing when he saw the smoke spreading out over the ground fifty yards up the hill. He did not ask Willie about it.

"I discovered that," Willie said, pointing to the smoke as it flowed close to the ground. "I don't know why it doesn't spiral upward through the trees. Not being able to see this place from down at the creek, and having the smoke go up the hill before it comes out, makes it impossible to spot the still until you get here."

Carl and Willie watched the thumper keg as it began to heat up. It was another learning experience for Carl. The lesson began as soon as they removed the sheet-metal covering the barrels. When they pulled the cloth coverings off of each barrel, Willie checked to see if the mash was ready to cook.

They skimmed off the 'head', a collection of grain and mold. Willie said, "A thick head on the mash means the 'shine will be smoother and stronger."

They saved everything they skimmed off and put it in a barrel. All the 'spent' grain would become hog feed.

The thumper was hot enough to make a noise. "It's beginning to thump," Willie said, referring to the noise from the pot of liquid. They had made sure the fermented liquid was free from debris. "The reason we strained all of the corn and grain out of the mash was to keep from stopping up the worm." Willie pointed to the small copper tubing twisted in a spiral above the thumper keg and winding its way downward toward a jug. There was steam coming out where the worm attached to the keg. "We have to vent it enough to keep it from exploding," Willie said as he showed him a safety peg that would blow if the worm became clogged.

Carl was convinced making moonshine was a lot of work and required a lot of patience. He knew the Sitton and Huckabee families made most of the 'shine along Big Creek. He didn't have an opinion about morality. He knew prohibition was because people blamed alcohol for a lot of problems. His family never had a drinking problem. Their beliefs and moral convictions were similar to Willie's. Carl's life at the bridge did not change his behavior.

He learned a lot about Willie after he married his daughter. Pauline loved her dad. She knew as soon as Carl came to live on the Sitton Homestead that Willie had plans for them. Her two older sisters didn't have a relationship similar to hers with Willie. Until Carl came, Willie had been taking her with him to feed cows and to do chores around the farm. Carl had replaced her. He was spending the time with Willie while she was cleaning the cabin and helping Ellen with household duties. Her role ended as a "tomboy".

She never got jealous of Carl for replacing her and taking away the time she spent with her dad. Carl thought about the discussions he had with Pauline about the moonshine business. She told him her mother would not discuss it. Preacher Ed came to see Willie when she was about six years old and she knew it was a special time. She remembered her mother talking about what a great change it would be if her dad became a Christian and started going to church.

Carl didn't understand what Pauline was saying when she talked about Preacher Ed converting Willie. He knew when he came up the creek looking for work, Preacher Ed had gotten drunk with Willie. There were people coming to the Harris homestead to pray for his mother during her illness. He remembered his dad asking some of them to leave his house after they accused him of being the reason his wife was dying. They didn't realize how deeply his dad was hurt when they accused him of being the reason she was dying and how much he wanted to see her healed.

"They told dad if he'd start going to church and doing what was right, Mom would be okay," Carl told Pauline during one of their discussions about Preacher Ed trying to convert Willie.

"They told Mama if Daddy didn't quit making moonshine, we would all die," Pauline said. "A bunch those folks died during that flu thing a few years before you came."

They sat silent and deep in thought after those discussions. As Carl remembered it, the discussions started after they discussed the shooting in Coy Bryant's barn.

He was amazed about how much she knew about Coy Bryant and her uncle's wife, Sister Rhodes', relationship before they were shot.

"Mama said when Uncle Jim married her, he knew she was a slut," Pauline told him. "Daddy also heard the story from Sheriff Joe Carson."

She went on to tell how Ellen Sitton would not let her eat at their house. While Jim Rhodes came really often to visit, he never brought Sister Rhodes with him. She remembered there was no conversation about the shooting between her mother and dad.

She told about overhearing Willie discussing the preacher knowing about Coy Bryant and his women with one of the Huckabee boys.

"Daddy and Preacher Ed talk about everything," Pauline said with a laugh. She explained, "I have played in the barn loft ever since I was little. Mama would send me after Daddy, and when he wasn't at the barn I would play in the loft until he came back. I would stay in the loft and be quiet while he brought someone in and made toddies." She paused. "They would be talking when they came to the barn. and I couldn't say anything because I would get in trouble for being there."

Carl listened, amazed as she told him the story. She went on to say, "I overheard Daddy tell Fred Hudson he was going to raise you like a son and he hoped someday you would marry me."

She told Carl she didn't like the idea when she overheard it. But as they got acquainted, she liked her daddy's idea. Carl could see from the very beginning what Willie had in mind. It started the first day he walked across the bridge. Carl thought about all that happened after he heard, "When you get to the bridge, Willie Sitton will put you to work; he always hires help." He wouldn't change a thing about his new life.

# CHAPTER 19

At the end of the day, when the mules were fed and before he walked home, Carl liked to stand on the bridge and watch the water flowing out of the "swimming hole". Sometimes he would sit at the end of the bridge and observe the structure.

Reviewing his life and the bridge seemed to go together. Building the bridge was a complicated mission. Carl's life had nowhere near as many details as the bridge. Supporting the bridge with the huge cables extending from concrete piers at each end was the first step in its construction. After the concrete piers were poured in place and the cables were attached, the bridge was all wood, except for the steel rods with an eye for the cable to run through and threads for fastening the timbers. Each one of the timbers of the bridge was fastened to the bolts with nuts and washers. The floor had joists running across the main timbers. There were thick oak boards making up the floor. The bridge side railings were fastened to the floor. The first chain-link fence ever used in the area made up the guardrails for the bridge.

Carl didn't know how to feel about his life. He really didn't own anything. When he started working there wasn't a set wage. His initial goal was to survive when he arrived at the bridge. Following Willie Sitton around and doing whatever he was asked to do became his duties. Now the moonshine business was the last thing he was learning. Before his trip to the still and mixing the mash, he was tending livestock, fixing water gates after a flood or cleaning the driftwood from the fields. Any extra time was spent cutting wood and working in the crops.

There were very few automobiles using the bridge. It was mostly wagons pulled by mules, and foot traffic. Willie made a good choice when he decided to build the barn at the end of the bridge.

Carl admired the bridge and the barn. It represented the place his new life started after he left the smoldering house where his mother and sister were buried. There were no regrets from staying behind when his dad and his sister left for Oklahoma.

While there were no regrets about being part of Willie Sitton's life, there were days when he missed the homestead and questioned his choice. Willie Sitton had taken control of his life. Did his desire to have a son cause him to adopt Carl? Only Willie could answer that.

It didn't matter, Carl shared most of Willie's ideas. It was easy for him to take control of Carl.

While Carl was thinking, he questioned if he had learned everything about the farm, he needed to know, and wondered why he was learning to make moonshine. Would he fire the forge in the blacksmith next? He believed he was being shaped in Willie Sitton's image. He got his answer very quickly about the blacksmith shop.

# CHAPTER 20

"**I** just want you to watch everything I do. Don't ask any questions," Willie said as Carl followed him to the blacksmith shop.

It made Carl wonder if Willie could read his mind. It was only a couple of days earlier when he was thinking about being shown everything except how to be a blacksmith.

He stood leaning against a post supporting the open side of the shop. The wall behind the forge and the wall next to the bridge were enclosed. The west end was open, and the south side had a wall four feet tall. Carl leaned against the post above the short wall. He watched Willie.

"I want you to watch me make a three-pronged pitch gig," Willie said.

He picked up a piece of metal almost one inch thick, and three inches wide by ten inches long.

"This is a piece of a road grader blade," he said as he laid it beside the forge.

Willie placed some shavings from a pine knot in the forge and lit them with a match. As the fire began to burn the pine shavings, he added lumps of coal. He explained that coal would not light immediately from a match. As the coal became hot from the flames, Willie slowly cranked the blower.

"I would let you crank the bellows and blow the air underneath the fire, but there's an art to how fast you crank, it has to be just right to get the lumps of coal to burn," Willie said as he started cranking and then slowed down to a very slow turn of the blower handle.

He cranked the handle until the lumps of coal were burning brightly. After the flames turned from yellow to a light blue, coming from the lumps of coal, he put the end of the metal into the fire. He used his hand to stick the metal into the burning flames of the coal.

"That's the last time I can touch the metal with my hand." Willie pulled a set of tongs off their hangers below the table of the forge. He held them up, showing them to Carl.

"These tongs are perfect for handling a pitch gig," he told Carl.

Carl watched as Willie continued to crank the bellows and the end of the metal turned red. As it got hotter the redness spread up the metal away from the flame. The end of the metal in the fire began to turn white. Willie removed it and placed it on the anvil. While he held the metal with the tongs, he placed it above a cutting chisel. Carl didn't notice when he dropped the cutting chisel with its square end inside the hole in the anvil. After placing the metal over the cutting chisel, he took a rather large hammer and hit it twice, splitting the end of the metal.

He moved it and attempted to split it again, then he turned and said to Carl, "I will have to heat up again before I can split the other side." He placed the metal back in the forge. Carl watched as it heated up once again.

The process of making the pitch gig was in its second

hour. The metal was heated and reheated several times. Each time a different step was started, the metal had to be white-hot and soft enough to be shaped. Each prong of the gig was beaten to a point and then spread apart and shaped. The middle prong remained straight in its original position. The two side prongs were first bent out at a 90° angle but then were curved to where they were about an inch apart at the points. Carl watched as Willie created all three of the points. He watched as he cut a little sliver on one side of the points making a beard. The beard was a portion of the gig which allowed it to hold a fish.

"I don't know why that thing's called a beard," Willie said after he made the three slices extended and shaped above the points. When he finished with the points, he heated it up to a temperature not quite as hot as it was while he was shaping it. He immediately stuck it into the water bucket by the anvil. "That's putting the temper into the metal. If it's too hard the prongs will break off as soon as you hit a rock"

He heated the gig one more time, and then stuck it into the water and left it until there was no steam coming out.

"I never know if I got it right until we get it on the shaft, and somebody throws it into the creek" Willie said as he held the gig up for Carl to examine.

Carl still did not understand how it was going to be attached to a handle.

Willie turned the gig around putting the other end into the fire. He heated just like he had the first time. He began pounding the metal on the anvil. He flattened the metal more each time he brought it out of the forge. When he had flattened it to about four inches in width, he got it warm enough to shape around the point of the anvil.

He began heating it, and each time he bent it farther around, creating a hollow pipe for the shaft of the handle. When he got it completely in a circle and had overlapped it, there was a hole for the handle. He then punched a small hole in each side of the metal. He finally stuck it in the water and let it cool, tempering the handle end of the gig.

Carl had been watching for over two hours. He wondered if he ever would have the patience to become a blacksmith. He also wondered why Willie was going to the trouble to teach him. He knew every spare minute Willie had was spent in the blacksmith shop. Most people said he wasn't working but was waiting for someone to come and pick up their moonshine.

Carl had never sold a jug of moonshine. He had been to the still and worked making 'shine. Now he had spent an afternoon in the blacksmith shop.

Just as they were leaving the blacksmith shop, Preacher Ed rode up on his little red mule.

"I stopped to ask you fellers to come to Hickory Sunday," Preacher Ed said as he got off the mule.

Neither Carl nor Willie answered immediately. They listened as the preacher explained they were going to have a special dinner and family day at the little church in Hickory Hollow. Willie agreed they would both be there without asking Carl.

# CHAPTER 21

The Hickory Hollow schoolhouse, a log building with a wood shingle roof, was a different structure from any of the other clapboard buildings built for schools. The Cedar Grove schoolhouse where Carl studied algebra was a boxed wall building with ship lap siding.

Carl and Pauline were seated in the second seat from the back, facing the podium. The seating was identical to Cedar Grove. The desks for students were still in place across the front of the building. The pews for seating the church crowd filled the back half of the room. A few folks were seated in the school desks.

Willie and Ellen Sitton were seated immediately behind the school desk. The singing continued. Carl wondered why Willie agreed to attend the church today. Preacher Ed stopped by the bridge quite often. He always shared a toddy with Willie, but they never drank more than two, and it was always made the same way as the whiskey used for colds. Carl wondered how much preacher Ed's conscience bothered him because he always looked away when he would take a sip of the toddy. He also knew it was a secret and he was to never share anything about the toddies.

Carl came into the room one afternoon when they were sharing a toddy and sneezed as he entered.

"We better fix you something for that before it gets any worse," Willie said as he placed the pot for heating the water back on the little stove. He added a couple of sticks of wood to the fire and Carl watched as he poured honey and 'shine into the water as it started to boil.

He laughed to himself after he drank the toddy, questioning why it was necessary that Preacher Ed and Willie drank one with him.

His mind flashed back to that afternoon while he was sitting in the church and listening to the songs.
Preacher Ed walked to the podium. He asked everyone to stand with him while he prayed an opening prayer before he delivered his sermon.

Carl had been to church a few times since he came to the Sitton Homestead. It was usually at Cedar Grove, where a fellow named Stephenson was the preacher. The reason why Preacher Ed didn't preach at the little schoolhouse close to the Big Creek bridge was never explained to Carl. While he was the pastor of the church at Big Flat, the one at Cozy and the one at Hickory, Pauline said they only went to Hickory if they knew Preacher Ed was going to be there.

Carl listened to the sermon. It was no different than any he had heard before, the few times he had ever attended church. He didn't know why the Harris family were never involved with religion. His mother had a Bible. Carl remembered her reading it a few times. He also remembered how irritated his dad became after his mother was sick and people insisted on praying for her and assuring his dad she would get well. When she didn't the disappointment was almost too much.

Preacher Ed talked about living a life acceptable to God.

He finished his sermon with a long dissertation along the lines of having respect for other people's lives. Carl thought about the conversations he overheard between Willie and Preacher Ed. While they would express opinions, he didn't remember them criticizing other people. Preacher Ed was smooth with his rhetoric. He talked about self-respect.

"Don't claim any righteousness if you don't respect your body, if you don't work enough to support yourself and your family, if you don't help your neighbor when he is in need, if you steal from your neighbor, and if you don't love your family and respect your children."

After that drawn-out list, Preacher Ed asked everyone to stand, and he prayed a blessing on all the food and those present who would enjoy their fellowship with their neighbors.

Carl watched as the food was uncovered and placed on the tables. He met several people for the first time. Anyone that shook hands with him immediately was able to tell him everything they knew about who he was. He was Willie Sitton's son-in-law, and they knew about his family and about the fire after his mother was buried.

He wondered how people could keep up with everybody else's business when he barely knew anyone except Preacher Ed and Willie Sitton.

He left the church and rode home in the back of the carriage. Willie was driving, and Pauline was sitting in the back seat next to him.

There was no conversation or opinions expressed about the sermon or the dinner. Carl wondered why Preacher Ed invited them to go. It was the first time since he went up the creek looking for work that he'd ever gone away from Big Creek to a social function of any kind.

# CHAPTER 22

Building a fire in the stove made sense to keep the chill out of the room next to the grain bin. The room was important for transacting business at the barn, and inside was the huge block of wood used as a poker table with the smaller cuts sitting around for stools.

Carl was looking for Willie when he opened the door and saw him adding wood to the fire.

"Come in," Willie greeted him as he entered the room.

It was unusual for Willie to speak to Carl. He usually looked at him and went back to whatever he was doing without saying anything.

Carl wondered if it had anything to do with them attending church at Hickory Hollow. It wasn't long before he got his answer.

"I wanted you to go with us to church yesterday," Willie said as he reached for the pot to start making toddies.

He poured water into it and set it on the stove.

"I need to explain why I wanted you to go," Willie began.

He spent the next few minutes explaining about the people who attended special church services.

"When there's a dinner at a church, a lot of men go, like me, that never attend any other time." He paused. "I go because I need to know how many of my 'shine buyers attend church."

He spent several minutes explaining how much he learned from observing his customers at a church service.

"First thing I see is whether or not they are embarrassed to see me there," Willie began, pouring the shine into the water as it got hotter.

Carl wondered if Willie was making a toddy for him or if he was planning to drink alone. Or was it possible that somebody else was coming to the barn?

While the water continued to heat, Willie continued with his explanation of what he learned as he observed people at the church functions.

"I get to see my customer's family," he said, and began to pour the toddies into the cups. "I can see if they are keeping shoes on their kids."

He handed Carl his cup. Carl was still standing, and Willie poured his own cup full, a lot more than he had given Carl. Willie sat down.

Carl sat down and still hadn't sipped anything from the cup. He didn't understand where this meeting and conversation was headed.

"We can't sell 'shine to people without money if they don't have enough character to take care of their family," Carl guessed.

"We don't make any money off of people around here," Willie said.

For the next several minutes he told the story about Jess Still falling off the bluff while he was 'coon hunting. He told Carl about everybody blaming him for his death. He had sold quite a bit of 'shine to him before he died. He told Carl about taking all the 'shine out of the barn and promising Ellen he would only sell the moonshine to people in cities. He talked about how good business was during prohibition. He talked about how much more money there was to be made during that period of time, and then he laughed.

"I got in trouble again." He stood up and poured more 'shine into his cup and looked at Carl's cup. Carl was not drinking much of his.

"John House got poisoned on some rotgut." Willie's eyes narrowed, and his face flushed as he started to tell the story of how he was blamed again for not furnishing good moonshine and letting his neighbor get poisoned.

Carl had heard those stories before, but it sounded different coming from Willie.

The next story Willie told Carl, while they were finishing the toddies, surprised him. He went into considerable detail about how Preacher Ed got started coming to the barn. He talked about how awkward it was for him to bring the preacher inside the room where he played poker and sold his moonshine. He told the story about the day, when he was aggravated about having the preacher there and decided to make a toddy to calm his nerves.

"As I watched the preacher and the expression on his face, I realized he was tempted by the toddy I was making." Willie stood up and walked around the room before he turned back to face Carl. "I regret what I did." With a pained expression, Willie paused "what's done is done".

He went on to explain how they drifted into their friendship. He talked about how much they realized they had in common. He never told Carl anything about the personal things he had discussed with Preacher Ed but when he finished telling the story, he added a detail.

"You came along during the time when Preacher Ed quit coming to see me. When he came to the mill where we were making molasses was the first time, I had seen him since he was drunk."

Carl still didn't understand the point of the visit. They

were interrupted by Newt Blair coming to pick up a quart of 'shine. Carl left the barn. He was left wondering what the conversation would've been like if they had finished. He loaded the wagon with hay and a couple of bags of grain to go up the creek and feed the calves they were weaning off the cows.

# CHAPTER 23

Carl fed the calves and didn't return to the barn that afternoon. There was a hole in the fence where one of the old cows was trying to get through to her calf. They carried wire and staples under the wagon seat to repair the fence. Carl spent most of the afternoon repairing the fence and trying to get one of the calves away from its mother.

He took the wagon back to the barn. Willie was nowhere around. He fed the mules and walked home as usual. He had not discussed anything about going to the still with Willie, or any of the discussions about why they went to church, with Pauline.

Carl became more like Willie the longer he lived and worked around him. Like Willie, he never discussed any of the business dealings on the farm with Pauline. Willie never told him to leave the women out of the farming, business but he just understood from being around Willie that none of their discussions were to ever be shared with Pauline's mother, or with Pauline.

He was late getting to the barn the next morning. Sometimes he didn't wake up early. It was one of those days. Willie was loading supplies for the still on the wagon when he walked into the hallway of the barn.

"Decided to come help me today?" Willie said with a laugh and pointed to the sacks of grain sitting on the wagon. "Move them further up front, so we'll have room for the rest of our stuff."

They finished loading the wagon, and then Willie was driving the mules. Carl had noticed when Willie didn't want to open gates, he would be in the seat of the wagon with the reins before Carl realized they were ready to go.

There wasn't anything said until they got even with the field where the Jayhawkers were buried.

"I know you've heard the story about my great uncle Eric shootin' them guys," Willie said as he pointed toward the monument. "It's hard to believe that he hid all that money for all of them years."

Willie was referring to the money belt Eric Huckabee found on the young boy riding with the other three men he killed that day.

"That happened in 1863 when he shot 'em," Willie continued his story. "We didn't find out where the guy was from until me and dad went to Colorado trying to find out where the horse he was riding came from."

Willie told Carl about how excited he was when he went with his dad to Colorado. He talked about all the whispering that was done between the family when they returned, and then he started describing how upset his great uncle Eric became when he realized he had killed the rancher's son. Willie continued the story telling Willie about how much he enjoyed helping Eric carve the monument for the grave.

Carl had heard all the stories before, but it sounded different coming from Willie. He was amazed how solemn Willie was when he talked about his uncle Eric. It was easy to figure out Eric Huckabee was Willie's hero. He expressed several times in several different ways how Eric was trustworthy.

"Can you imagine having $14,000 dollars hidden underneath the corn crib for all of them years?"

Willie ended the discussion and continued driving the mules toward the still. Carl was waiting for Willie to renew the conversation they were having before Newt Blair interrupted them, but he never did.

# CHAPTER 24

Carl listened to Willie every time he referred to his great uncle, Eric Huckabee. Stories told along Big Creek seldom changed. The shooting of the Jayhawkers and Eric hiding the money belt after for all those years was one of the favorite stories people enjoyed telling.

When they got to the still, Carl began cleaning out the mash barrels. Willie was particular about cleaning the barrels.

"They've got to be cleaner than the pan does before we cook the juice from the cane," Willie said, referring to the sorghum mill and making molasses.

There wasn't much conversation as they scrubbed the barrels. They turned them upside down to drain. Willie took a brown paper sack from underneath the wagon seat.

"Here's a biscuit with sausage." He handed it to Carl. "Is Pauline a good cook?"

Carl thought a minute before he answered, "yeah," but he didn't add any details and Willie never asked another question.

They ate lunch in silence. Carl liked not having to continually carry on a conversation with Willie. From the stories he heard about Willie when he was young, he went from a continuous flow of questions as a kid to a slow talker as an adult. They eventually returned to the discussion of Eric Huckabee.

"Coming down the creek by the marker me and uncle Eric made has got me to thinking about him." Willie stood up and walked down to the ledge looking off into Big Creek and the mouth of Bratton Creek. "Uncle Eric was happy living on Big Creek. I don't know why he didn't fight in the Civil War."

Willie was continuing with the rambling dialogue about Eric Huckabee as he walked back from the ledge overlooking the mouth of Bratton. His thoughts and what he was saying didn't make sense to Carl.

"Life's full of choices. He chose to follow his sweetheart from Wayne County Tennessee to Big Creek. If the Blairs had stayed in Tennessee, I would've never gotten acquainted with my great uncle Eric." Willie sat back down on the wagon. He was in no hurry to turn the mash barrels over and start mixing the mash.

He went into a lengthy description about Eric Huckabee. He described him as the best craftsman he ever met. He talked about how the tools in the Huckabee toolshed were hung in order, and not any of them out of place.

"Uncle Eric taught me early on that if you spent time looking for one of your tools, it was your fault." He went back to the wagon and took out another paper bag. He handed Carl a chocolate roll. He didn't say anything, they just began eating their desserts. "I believed everything Uncle Eric told me."

Willie was not finished with his description of his great uncle. Noah Sitton, Willie's grandfather, was married to Eric Huckabee's sister. Carl had learned over the last several years most of the things Willie wanted him to know about Pauline's family. Willie had described how they worked hard, shared everything within the family, and took care of the neighbors.

The story about Willie quitting selling 'shine because Jess Still fell off the bluff, and then starting to 'sell shine again because John House got poisoned on rotgut, was Carl's favorite story, but now he was learning things about the philosophy behind what Willie Sitton believed.

Willie believed money was necessary, but it was more important to be self-sufficient and grow your own food and take care of the things needed to live. When he finished telling him what he believed about his uncle Eric, Carl understood why they returned the money to Colorado. He understood the belief that success depended on self-sufficiency. Carl understood how particular Pauline was with their clothes. It was all part of the philosophy Willie had been sharing for the last year.

They began filling the mash barrels.

"I'll let you put the grain in," Willie said as they began unloading the supplies from the wagon. "You remember what goes in first?"

Carl didn't answer. Instead, he started putting the same amount of corn in each barrel as before. He mixed the wheat and oats together and put them in after the corn. Willie began running the water into the barrels. Carl didn't ask or say anything, he just started adding the wheat shorts to the barrels after Willie finished filling each one with water. Carl didn't add sugar to the wheat shorts. He didn't retrieve the starter cake from the barrel next to the thumper keg.

He remembered. He knew Willie had watched him and every move he had made after they started filling the mash barrels.

"I wonder if I've done it right," Carl questioned himself.

He got his answer.

"Carl, you're going to make it. For whatever it's worth,

you're going to be able to make good 'shine." Willie gave him his approval.

They covered the barrels with cloth, tying the cloth down and then they placed the metal roofing covers over the barrels before they weighted it down with rocks.

Willie was quiet all the way back home. He rode as a passenger in the wagon. He opened the gates.

Carl watched him. He always wondered what was going through Willie's mind. Was he thinking about Preacher Ed and all the gossip people spread about their drinking? Was he remembering things he discussed with the preacher before Coy Bryant and Sister Rhodes were shot? Was he feeling guilty about his relationship with preacher Ed. Did Willie question himself about other things? Like teaching Carl to make moonshine.

Carl didn't know what Willie's thoughts were about. Meanwhile He was learning a lot of skills in addition to learning how to make moonshine. Besides that, he also developed the philosophy of making a living on Big Creek.

# CHAPTER 25

The 1920swere described as the roaring 20s. There was never much change around the Sitton Homestead and when Prohibition ended, the only effect was less demand for moonshine. Bonded legal whiskey was replacing moonshine but the taste for bourbon bottled in Kentucky was not developed enough to replace the 'shine made along the bluffs around Big Flat Arkansas.

Willie and Carl were still mixing mash and running moonshine, but not as much as years before. They were not making any runs of whiskey until the stock at the barn got low enough to need replenishment.

Preacher Ed Tice and Willie Sitton were the best-known people in the area. Carl Harris was Willie Sitton's son-in-law. His reputation as a surrogate for Willie was becoming widespread.

"If Willie is not around, just see Carl," was a common quotation.

The clouds were low. It was turning colder. The wind was

changing from the south to the north.

"Better get all the stock fed and meet me at the barn," Willie said as Carl headed up the creek with several bales of hay.

December was early to be feeding as much hay as they were. It was a dry fall. The fields where the cattle grazed were eaten bare. It was going to be a tough winter on Big Creek.

It was almost dark when Carl joined Willie at the barn. He put the wagon under the shed and fed the mules before he went into the barn. He could hear the water beginning to boil. Willie was making a toddy. It had become their habit. Willie and Carl did not drink enough liquor to be a problem. Willie had insisted early on, "if you learn the moonshine business, the most important thing is to not drink too much your product."

Carl believed that. Also, Pauline was Willie's favorite child, and she wanted Carl to be as much like their dad as possible. Carl never understood that when he first arrived at Big Creek. He didn't know when it was that he realized Willie had cultivated him as a son.

Carl went into the room which was filled with the smell of the honey added to the water on the stove. He liked the pungent odor. He almost stepped on Preacher Ed before he saw him sitting in the corner. It was late. He wondered why the preacher was there so late in the afternoon.

"I left my horse here this morning and rode in a car with a neighbor to Marshall," Preacher Ed explained. "That was early. I planned on being back by two o'clock this afternoon."

Willie poured the 'shine into the water that was boiling with the honey. He poured a lot more than usual.

"That ole' car broke down about halfway up the hill coming out of that barren hollow," the preacher continued his story.

Willie poured all three of them a cup of the toddy. They

began to sip while the preacher continued to explain how hard it was to get back to Big Creek. He had ridden with three different wagons and finally the storekeeper at Hickory brought him to the bridge in his buggy.

"Carl, how long has it been since you came here to the bridge?" the preacher asked.

"I got here in the spring before the shooting that next October, whenever that was," Carl answered, without explicitly referring to Coy Bryant or Sister Rhodes.

"You came right after your mother died?" Preacher Ed asked. Willie sat quietly and did not enter the conversation. "I meant to come see her, while she was sick." Preacher Ed continued.

There was a long period of silence. Carl didn't know how to get into a discussion about things which happened when he was just a boy. His memories of the period of time before his mother died were tormenting.

"Do you remember people coming to pray for your mother?" Preacher Ed asked.

Carl didn't answer for a few minutes. He thought about when people came one evening and asked his dad if they could pray. He remembered his dad being excited and telling them he would be glad if they would. He remembered the first night. Only, his dad thought they would pray a prayer and leave, but the people stayed. One man walked a circle continuously back and forth around his mother's bed. Carl was a twelve-year-old boy. He did not understand. They were loud and it was time for him and his sister to go to bed.

He couldn't remember all that happened. He remembered taking his camping quilt his mother had just finished and going to the barn to sleep. He remembered coming back the next morning and there being four more people there. It made a total of seven people in their house praying for his mother.

He remembered his dad getting irritated and eventually running them off before bedtime the second night.

"Yes," Carl finally answered Preacher Ed.

Willie spoke up.

"Them was good people." Willie didn't wait for preacher Ed and Carl to continue the conversation. He went into a description of how the group of people who came to pray for Carl's mother believed in miracles. He talked about how his mother believed in prayer and faith. Carl was shocked. Willie taught him everything he knew about running a farm. Willie taught him to make moonshine. Willie insisted they sell shine to people who were not drunks. He was convinced Willie believed that his moonshine business filled an important purpose along Big Creek. He never knew how deep the convictions were about religion until Willie finished defending the people who prayed for his mother. Carl thought about how much his life had changed since his mother died. Willie was right. Everybody would've been pleased if after their prayers his mother had gotten well.

"I don't know anything about that, I was just a boy." Carl stood up, walked over to the pot on the stove and poured the last of its contents into his cup. He never drank but one toddy at a time. Today was different.

"My mother died. My dad lost faith in people and himself. Before we came to Arkansas, we lived in the extreme northeast corner of Mississippi. That little corner of mountains north of the Tennessee River," Carl continued.

Maybe it was the extra 'shine he drank from the second cup, but he spent quite a bit of time explaining to preacher Ed how his family never knew anything about religion. He told about how they lived at the upper end of a creek coming out of the mountains. He told the preacher about how many times you had to wade the creek to get to a schoolhouse and a church service. He never learned anything about the Bible or religion. He knew they wanted his mother and his sister to live. The hardest part of their experience with the people who prayed for his mother was when they told them that she was dying because they were heathens. Carl never understood how they could be blamed for his mother's death.

Preacher Ed walked over toward Carl. He stood there looking down at Carl as he was sitting in the opposite corner from where he was before. Willie started to interrupt and say something, but he changed his mind.

They listened as Preacher Ed explained how hard it was to know the truth. How hard it is to keep from judging other people and their ideas. How hard it is to keep from failing. He told Carl most of the story of his life. He too, grew up with a father who didn't see the need for religion but never fought against the family going to church. He finally ended what he was saying to Carl by adding, "I don't know how I've become what I am."

He turned away from Carl and looked out the door as he opened it, as if he was about to leave. He closed the door and came back in. He stopped in the middle of the room, and he towered above the poker table. His head almost brushed against the joist holding up the roof. He looked down at Carl before saying, "The most important thing I've learned through all my failures is to respect other people in their failures."

The preacher went to the barn loft to spend the night. Carl and Willie went to their houses. The discussion ended.

# CHAPTER 26

The horse pulling the buggy was going at a faster pace. Willie was driving. Carl joined him and Preacher Ed for breakfast after Willie blew the fox horn. It was an emergency signal, and it awakened Carl. Pauline was still in bed when Carl came back in and told her it wasn't an emergency. Willie just yelled, "Come to breakfast!".

They were on a trip to Marshall to the hardware store. It wasn't a planned trip. After preacher Ed left, Willie counted the blank horseshoes. He decided they needed to go pick up enough to last for a while.

Carl would have to feed the livestock when they got back. Willie wasn't talking much. Carl decided to start a conversation about automobiles.

"Do you think we ought to get a car?'' Carl asked.

He knew Willie's opinion about automobiles. He had listened to stories about people coming to buy 'shine that couldn't get their car to start when they got ready to leave. He also heard Willie telling another story about a guy getting cracked in the head by the crank when the car backfired. Carl saw a fellow in Big Flat with a broken arm. After the guy left, Jim Rhodes told the story about how he broke it. "He got his arm broke while he was trying to crank a car!"

"No," Willie finally answered Carl's question. Carl waited for him to continue and explain his reasons for the answer.

Willie went into a long story about how many times he had known of people having to rent a horse and a buggy to get home when their car tore up. He told the story again about the car preacher Ed drove sometimes.

"A feller gave that car to Preacher Ed when he went back to Ohio" Willie said.

Carl regretted asking. He wondered if Willie would ever own one. Pauline was beginning to want a car because a lot of their friends were talking about getting an automobile.

They rode the rest of the way to Marshall in silence. They tied the horse up next to the watering trough and walked up the hill to the hardware store.

"Carl, you get the blank horseshoes. Get three sizes for mules. Get several sizes for saddle horses. We don't need many of the work shoes for horses."

Carl wasn't sure he knew enough about the horseshoes to buy them. Willie had only let him work once or twice in the blacksmith shop while they were shaping horseshoes to fit. He knew a mule shoe was narrow and straighter than the ones for the saddle horses. He also knew the shoes for work horses were huge and had a toe and heel plate already on them. He decided to ask for help.

"Willie needs to restock all of the horseshoes" he told the stock boy at the hardware store. The clerk knew exactly what Willie always bought. He put them in a wooden crate. Carl decided they would have to bring the buggy and pick them up. They were too heavy. He was not going to carry them down the hill to where the buggy was parked.

He looked around for Willie and saw him standing across

the courtyard next to the courthouse, visiting with a tall, well-dressed man. Carl walked up and joined them.

"Carl, this is Alan Bryant," Willie introduced him without mentioning he was the brother of Coy Bryant. Carl didn't join the conversation. He decided to go to the fabric store and surprise Pauline by picking up some fabric to make him some new shirts from dark denim. He liked the look and color of the shirts Ellen had been making for Willie.

After he paid for the cloth, he started walking toward the buggy. While shifting the cloth from his right hand to left, he turned and watched a rider going away from the courthouse. He recognized the rider as Alan Bryant and was in shock when he saw the horse. His eyes stayed fixed on the horse as it went out of sight. It was a flashback to the rider and horse he had seen leaving the barn after the shooting.

The rest of the walk toward the buggy was spent searching his memory of a chestnut horse with a dark tail and a man leaning forward while riding at a full gallop. It was all he remembered seeing as they were going over the hill away from the barn. It had been years, and he wasn't sure he would recognize the horse if he ever saw it again. He was wrong. His mouth was dry as he tried to think of what he had just seen. By the time he got to the buggy, he decided he wasn't saying a word.

The horseshoes were loaded. Willie was a constant chatter as he tried to tell Carl about all the gossip he had picked up while visiting at the courthouse. There were federal revenue agents trying to locate moonshine stills. Sheriff Joe Carson had assured Willie they would never find their way to Big Creek. Carl didn't really listen. He was too busy trying to reconcile what he saw when Alan Bryant rode away from the courthouse.

# CHAPTER 27

Pauline insisted Carl go to Big Flat with her to have some shirts made by the dressmaker. Carl liked the shirts the dressmaker made for Willie, especially the collar and the new cuffs. She wanted Carl to have some just like those. They took the buggy, and it was an easy trip to Big Flat. They got there before noon.

Carl stopped the buggy and let Pauline out at the dress shop. She had the material he bought for his shirts, plus she also had three more pieces of cloth. There was no discussion what the extra pieces of cloth were for.

"I'm going up to the store for preacher Ed to cut my hair," Carl said before he pulled away with the buggy.

He tied the horse to the hitching post and went into the store. There wasn't anybody in the area of the barber's chair. He was walking through the store when he met Preacher Ed.

"You are cutting hair today?" he asked.

Preacher Ed didn't answer the question. He took the papers he had in his hand and laid them next to the cash register.

"Come on." He motioned to Carl and went to the barber's chair.

He had only cut Carl's hair twice before. Pauline had been cutting his hair since he got to the bridge.

There was no conversation. He was trimming the edges with scissors and a comb.

"I got these new clippers; they don't seem to work very well." He flexed the handles back and forth and put some oil on the blades. "Do you want me to try 'em?"

Carl nodded and leaned back on the chair. The clippers were cutting smoothly, and Carl did not feel any pulling of his hair.

Seth Tabor from Cozy came in while preacher and was cutting Carl's hair.

He spoke before taking a seat next to the window. "How are you fellers today?"

Carl recognized him. He had heard the stories about how many times Seth was questioned about the shooting at Coy's barn. He guessed Seth had answered more questions than anyone. Sheriff Joe Carson had questioned both.

Preacher Ed stepped back from the chair and stopped cutting Carl's hair.

"What are you doing in Big Flat today, Seth?" Preacher Ed asked.

"I dropped Melissa off at the dress shop as usual," Seth answered. "She wants Ms. Rorie to make the boy some shirts."

Carl did mention that Pauline was also at the dress shop. While they knew Seth and Melissa when they saw them, they had never visited with them or even been in the same room.

Preacher Ed seemed uncomfortable. Carl wondered if Preacher Ed's mind was racing, trying to remember all the conversations he and Willie had about the murders of Coy Bryant and Sister Rhodes. It only took a few minutes until Carl got his answer.

"You two men know more about what happened years ago at the barn than anybody," Preacher Ed began, without referring to the shooting directly. "You both saw the horse and rider leave the barn."

Carl noticed how quickly Seth looked at him when Preacher Ed said that. He didn't respond. Seth didn't, either. Carl thought back to a few days earlier when he watched Alan Bryant ride up the hill away from the courthouse at Marshall. He hoped his face didn't show any expression, but he wondered about the looks Seth gave him and the wry smile on his face.

When they didn't make any comment, Preacher Ed dropped the subject. He finished cutting Carl's hair. Carl went to the back of the store and began looking at the different jars of hard candy. He got two small bags and filled each one half-full. When he looked around for a clerk, he realized Preacher Ed was running the store by himself. He went back and sat down in the chair where Seth was sitting before.

"That boy of yours and Melissa's has got that red hair," Preacher Ed said to Seth. They all three laughed together when they remembered the story everybody told about Seth and Melissa saying, "The boy's hair better be red."

It lightened the moment and the conversation turned to how fast the boy was growing. He was going to be a husky lad. Seth began telling stories about how hard a worker he was and how smart he was in school.

They both asked Carl when he was going to have a kid. Carl did not answer. He left the store after he paid for the candy and went to find Pauline.

While they were riding home in the buggy, Pauline told him about her conversation with Melissa. He couldn't believe they had discussed that he and Seth were the only two witnesses to the shooter leaving the barn.

Pauline asked. "Have you and Seth ever discussed that?"

Carl didn't answer. He was sure they would never discuss

the horse or who the rider was. He would never repeat anything about what he thought. Pauline changed the subject and they drove home in silence. It was a good trip to Big Flat. Carl liked the time he spent getting better acquainted with Seth Tabor. He knew whatever they knew, it would always be between them.

# CHAPTER 28

Carl listened as the water sizzled from the hot horseshoe being submerged into it. Willie decided it was time to teach Carl how to shape and fit horseshoes. Carl enjoyed working in the blacksmith shop. At first, he didn't like working with the hot metals and hammering on the anvil. Now he was used to the hammering and was amazed how long he could stand and crank the bellows. It allowed him to think about other things while the metal was getting hot. It had been a few weeks since he saw Seth Tabor at Big Flat.

Since seeing Seth, Carl had given a lot of thought to the expression on his face when Preacher Ed made the comment about them being the only ones who saw the horse and rider at the barn that day. A week or so after seeing Seth in Big Flat, Carl saw him in Marshall. Willie had sent him to pick up supplies at the hardware store. He was in a hurry to get back before a storm hit, and truthfully, he didn't want to talk to Seth. He purposely avoided talking to Seth.

Carl wondered if Seth had seen Alan Bryant's horse after

the day of the shooting. His thoughts continued to wonder after he got home and was working in the blacksmith shop.

After the distracting memory, he was heating the horseshoe for the third time. He continued trying to shape the horseshoe and get the curve right. The horse was in the corral waiting for the shoe. The shoe had to be shaped just right before it was put on the horse. The shoe he removed from the horse was being used as the pattern for shaping the replacement. Willie had helped Carl remove several shoes from the horses. If they were not well-fitted, Willie showed him the corrections that needed to be made on the replacements. The shoes for this horse didn't need any correction, Willie had been replacing the shoes on it since it was a colt.

"Make sure you take the old shoe off first, then use it as a pattern to shape the new one. Don't try to put the shoe on the horse until you get it shaped right," were always Willie's instructions.

Seth Tabor's mules were in the corral when Carl got to the barn. He didn't know where Willie had gone for the day but he found a note telling him to get the shoes off of Seth's mules and trim their hooves, and then to do his best to get the shoes ready for the mules.

Willie added a P.S. to the note. "Seth will be here tomorrow. It will probably take all three of us to put the shoes on his mules."

It was harder to shape a mule shoe. They were straighter and could only be worked in the toe area. They had to be held by the tongs on one side and shaped over the horn of the anvil. It was much easier working on the bigger shoes for the workhorses. Carl enjoyed shaping the shoes for the saddle horses.

While he continued heating the shoes in the forge, his thoughts went back to Seth's expression when Preacher Ed commented about them being the only people who saw the horse and rider leaving the shooting. He wondered again, as he had for the past few days, if Seth had recognized Alan Bryant as the rider.

Tomorrow was a day he dreaded. Being around Seth would be easy, but would Willie start asking more questions while they put shoes on the mules? He knew Willie. He was just like Preacher Ed. Carl was working on the harness when he overheard their conversation with Seth. They were expressing their theories about the shooting. He remembered making sure that he heard every word. He felt silly holding his ear next to a crack in the wall between the room and the tack room while he listened to their conversation. He never repeated what he heard, nor had he asked any questions.

# CHAPTER 29

Carl was late getting to the barn the next morning. Seth was there with Wille. They were trying to match the shoes to the mules. Willie ignored him when he walked up to the corral. Over the years, he had learned if Willie was unhappy or disappointed with something he had done or was doing, his response was to ignore him. Carl found out early on not to say a word, just step in and start doing his job until Willie decided he wanted to talk. Willie picked up one of the mule's shoes.

"That's the wrong shoe for this mule," Willie said after he looked at the shoe.

"How was we supposed to know which set of shoes goes with which mule?" Willie's question ended with a smile.

"I thought the mules would tell you," Carl said, and Willie and Seth both laughed.

Putting the mule shoes on went a lot smoother than expected. There wasn't any conversation about anything during the time they were working with the mules. They were just trying to get the job done. Carl clinched the nails after Willie drove them through the hooves. He held a flat piece of metal against the bottom of the shoe and used a chisel to cut the nail off before the shoe was clinched to the hoof. It was the first time Willie had asked him to do the clinching. Usually, Willie insisted on nailing the shoe onto the animal, and also clinching the nails to the hoof.

The job was done. They stopped for lunch after the mules were shod, and Carl didn't see who brought the lunch. After the mules were tied to the hitching rail in front of the barn, Willie said "let's eat' as he walked into the area where the poker games were held. They ate in silence. Carl hoped there would not be any discussion with Seth about the shooting. He was getting tired of the questions after all these years at the barn.

Willie had been giving them both a questioning stare while they ate.

"I am not going to start the discussion about what you two fellers saw." he said, hoping his comment would get the discussion started.

Neither Seth nor Carl commented.

Willie could not resist talking about the day the shooting occurred. It was the first time he had both witnesses together with him in the barn. He went into a long dissertation about how any discussion now was useless. He went into detail about all the different theories over the last few years concerning who murdered Coy Bryant and Sister Rhodes. He continued sharing some wild ideas, but, neither Carl nor Seth said anything in response to Willie's comments. Willie got water and began to heat it on the stove. It was obvious he was going to prepare a toddy for them.

Carl wondered if Preacher Ed would show up around the time the water got hot, but he didn't. The conversation did not return to Seth and Carl being witnesses to the rider leaving the barn.

He was relieved. He believed Willie when he said, "Any

discussion now won't mean a thing."

Whatever Carl and Seth saw could not be verified. The impossibility of Alan Bryant being able to be at the barn at the right time to do the shooting was a good defense.

It would have taken a collaboration between him and Coy Bryant's wife. Then who would have carried the word between them? How did anyone know when Coy and Sister Rhodes planned to meet? Carl wondered if Seth was having the same thoughts as he was. He wondered if Seth had ever recognized Alan Bryant's horse.

He was done with it. After they finished putting the shoes on the mules and after they finished eating, he doubted he would ever have another good reason for spending time with Seth.

He questioned if Willie had wanted him to be a part of putting shoes on Seth's mules to get an opportunity to ask more questions. If that was the plan, he wondered why Willie thought it would work. Without saying what he was trying to do, Carl thought he tried a really sly way of giving him and Seth an opportunity to jump into the conversation. Neither one of them said a word.

Willie stood with Carl as they watched Seth leave the barn. He was riding one of the mules and leading the other. He didn't make any comment about Seth except to say, "He's almost as good a worker as you are, Carl."

Willie turned then and went inside the barn. Carl followed him. He listened while Willie reminisced about the time after he got to the bridge.

When Willie finished talking about that period of time, he added, "We have had two things happen that changed our lives, your mother dying and you coming here to work." After pausing for a moment, he continued, "I will add one more thing—you witnessed the shooting."

Willie began adding to Carl's story by explaining how pleased he was with all the things Carl had learned. He began listing things, including farm work, feeding the cows, making moonshine, working in the blacksmith shop, and on and on about every phase of the work on the Sitton Homestead.

Carl wasn't sure why Willie was talking about the things they'd accomplished. Carl liked hearing the compliments, but he smiled when he thought about Willie, not ever mentioning he always planned on him becoming his son-in-law. Carl left the barn and went home to the cabin which was now his and Pauline's house. It was a good day.

# CHAPTER 30

The sun warmed Carl quickly in the morning as he sat on the porch. It was the same place where he always sat, a corner that was created on the east side of the house when the porch was expanded and was always out of the wind. From this point the view of the hill was perfect for watching the sunrise. The shadows always moved up the hollow as the sun rose higher above the hill. A small stream flowed past the house. The spring at the base of the hill was the water supply for the house and fed the stream. Drinking coffee while watching the animals was one of Carl's favorite things.

While spending evenings sitting with Pauline in the same corner on the porch was also one of Carl's favorite times. It wasn't a place for conversation, they preferred to sit in silence as the shadows crept up from the creek.

The sounds at dusk were totally opposite from the sounds at dawn. Squirrels from the mornings were replaced by the raccoons that worked the stream at night. They were catching crayfish for their evening meal. A fox would come down the hollow occasionally and Carl had watched one catch a rabbit just below the house. As darkness settled in, there was nothing to see as the sounds of the night increased.

Winter mornings were silent. The noise in the spring with the birds singing always reminded Carl of when he left the burning house to go up the creek. Noises always carried memories for Carl, whether it was the dripping of the water from the limbs of the cedars or the sound of a mink catching a fish. All the sounds brought back memories of days gone by. The sound of gravel crunching underneath Cal Morrow's feet was one of the better memories. All of the memories were in the distant past, but this morning he was thinking about the recent days.

The discussions with Willie and Seth were lingering in his mind. He was continuing to think and compare the conversations with Willie and Seth to those with Willie and Preacher Ed.

*"I think I have a better understanding of everyone, including Willie and Preacher Ed,"* he thought. The recalling of events since he got to the bridge caused Carl to take a better look at himself.

Was he happy? Was he successful? The answer to those questions usually depended on the comparisons being made to other people. Who could Carl compare his life to?

The answer to the question began with his being a part of the Sitton family. A look at the family history was needed to understand his part. The homestead was almost one hundred years old. Noah Sitton decided not to settle in the Campbell community with Ethan Massey, his lifelong friend, had chosen a better spot to settle than a bluff above Big Creek. The land where Ethan settled was deep rich soil.

While the Sitton homestead was on a bluff with very shallow soil on the bench land, it also included land along the banks of Big Creek. The land next to the creek was made up of narrow bottoms with deep, fertile soil, but flooded every spring. Sometimes a flood would occur just after a crop was planted. It meant the work had to be done over immediately.

Carl and Pauline Harris were part of the fourth generation since the Sitton Homestead began. Willie was third generation and was probably the most successful homesteader in the area. Whether it was making moonshine, cutting crossties during the railroad construction period, or just being a good manager, he was successful.

The lessons Carl had learned since coming up the creek were to be expected. "If you can get to the bridge, Willie Sitton will hire you," they had said. They had been right.

A statement more than a question came to mind. Yes, Carl went to work and considered himself a success. As he looked back over the years, he realized Willie Sitton did not hire him to work. He adopted him to become his son-in-law. What was success? You might say, "it is when an opportunity comes along, and you are able to take advantage of it."

Carl did not like that definition. He was happy. He had just learned during breakfast that Willie Sitton was going to become a grandfather.

Their lives were about to change, and Carl was sure he was finished with his training as a moonshiner.

# ABOUT THE AUTHOR

Sam Pemberton was born on Bratton Creek, at an old homestead that hadn't changed much since the pioneer days. The year was 1944. Pemberton graduated from Big Flat high school. After their graduation in 1962, Sam married the love of his life, Patricia Treat.

He has worked construction in the drywall trade for most of his life. Sam presently lives in the beautiful Ozarks and continues in construction. He loves writing his stories and enjoys his morning coffee and porch time.

# OTHER BOOKS BY SAM PEMBERTON

The Moonshiner and the Preacher
Finding Big Flat
Zeek's Journey to Freedom
Missy's Life as a Slave
Moonshiner the Witness
Livin' Under Goldies Rule

www.ingramcontent.com/pod-product-compliance
Lightning Source LLC
Chambersburg PA
CBHW060940120626
46557CB00003B/1080